THE Disappearance OF Lady Edith

THE UNDAUNTED DEBUTANTES
Book 1

CHRISTINA McKNIGHT

PRAISE FOR CHRISTINA MCKNIGHT'S NOVELS

THE THIEF STEALS HER EARL

"When I started reading this book I could not put it down...it caused another book-hangover for me. I wanted to see how things would go when the truth of Judith came out and how Simon was going to handle it...loved it."-*Sissy's Book Review*

"Jude and Cart's story is such a delight! So refreshing to see the hero shy, socially awkward and not super wealthy. I love it...This was definitely one of the best books I've read this summer." -*Reviews from a Thrifty Mom*

FORGOTTEN NO MORE

"This author has made me love historical romance again."
-*TwinsieTalk Book Reviews*

HIDDEN NO MORE

"The storyline was really good, the writing was great. So smooth and engaging, I was able to zip right through the story, it flowed so well. I love finding new to me authors and with this wonderfully written story by Ms. McKnight I've found a new historical romance author."-*Bound by Books*

CHRISTMAS EVER MORE

"*Christmas Ever More* was a wonderfully written festive novella full of hope, renewal, love, and new beginnings. If you're a fan of Christina's Lady Forsaken series, this is a must. Even if you aren't caught up, this stands well enough on its own to be a lovely addition to your holiday reading list."-*Literal Addiction*

BOOKS BY CHRISTINA MCKNIGHT

The Undaunted Debutantes Series
The Disappearance of Lady Edith
The Misfortune of Lady Lucianna
The Misadventures of Lady Ophelia

Lady Archer's Creed Series
Theodora
Georgina
Adeline – August 2017
Josephine – November 2017

Craven House Series
The Thief Steals Her Earl
The Mistress Enchants Her Marquis
The Madame Catches Her Duke – Coming Soon
The Gambler Wagers Her Baron – Coming Soon

A Lady Forsaken Series
Shunned No More
Forgotten No More
Scorned Ever More
Christmas Ever More,
Hidden No More, A Lady Forsaken

Standalone Titles
The Siege of Lady Aloria, A de Wolfe Pack Novella
A Kiss At Christmastide
For The Love Of A Widow

DEDICATION

To Marc
Thank you for your unwavering support and love!

ACKNOWLEDGMENTS

There are several people I'd like to thank for staying with me through the hectic journey of writing this book.

To Marc, my amazing boyfriend—thank you for always being *you*!

To Lauren Stewart, my critique partner and best friend, you pushed me to explore new avenues of thought that I never dreamed possible. If we were in a true relationship, it would be one based on co-dependency, but in a good way. My writing would not be what it is without your comments, criticism, suggestions, and guidance.

I'd also like to thank the wonderful women who've supported me in both my writing career and life, including (but not limited to): Erica Monroe, Amanda Mariel, Debbie Haston, Angie Stanton, Theresa Baer, Ava Stone, Roxanne Stellmacher, Laura Cummings, Dawn Borbon, Suzi Parker, Jennifer Vella, Brandi Johnson, and Latisha Kahn. I know I'm forgetting people…You have all been very patient and wonderfully supportive of my eccentric ways.

A very special thank you to my editor, Chelle Olson with Literally Addicted to Detail, your skill and professionalism surpass all that I expected. Chelle Olson can be contracted by email at literallyaddictedtodetail@yahoo.com.

Also, a special thank you to historical and developmental editor, Scott Moreland.

And to my proofreader, Anja, thank you for embarking on yet another journey with me.

Cover design by The Midnight Muse.

Wraparound cover design credit to Sweet 'N Spicy Designs.

Finally, thank *you* for supporting indie authors.

PROLOGUE

Devonshire, England
December 1813

As it sounded its final gong, Lady Edith Pelton glanced at the towering, mahogany clock nestled between two bay windows overlooking the dark gardens below. The fire in the hearth had long been reduced to nothing but glowing embers.

However, the chill that had settled on the room hadn't been noticed.

"I truly must return to my chambers before His Grace suspects I have slipped out...before our marriage was so much as consummated." Lady Tilda Abercorn, formally Miss Tilda Guthton—the lowly daughter of a mere baronet—leapt to her feet from the lounge she shared with her dearest companions. That very morning, she'd wed the Duke of Abercorn, becoming a duchess.

And the envy of her three bosom friends.

Edith laughed along with the other two women, Lady Ophelia and Lady Lucianna, as they stood, all prepared to send Tilda off to her waiting marriage bed, her new husband, and the delights certain to await her.

Not that Edith or her friends knew anything about

what awaited Tilda behind those closed doors; however, this hadn't stopped them from gossiping about it for the past hour.

They likely would have remained ensconced in the salon had the tall clock not chimed twelve…it was even now five minutes past midnight.

Tilda was rightfully anxious; innocent and demure, much like Edith and their two other friends. She'd asked them to meet her after everyone else retired, not because she was avoiding her marriage bed—certainly not. She'd simply needed to draw a measure of confidence from those who cared most for her.

The hour was scandalously late; however, it meant all the other guests had retired to their beds. As such, it would be much easier for Edith and her friends to go unnoticed as they made their ways to their own rooms. The darkened household gave them the perfect opportunity for a few private moments with Tilda before she departed to France for her bridal tour with her new husband. It was unlikely the couple would return before the end of the Season.

"You will tell us everything on the morrow? At breakfast, and not a moment later. I truly must know if everything is as I've been told." Lady Lucianna raised one brow suggestively. Her green eyes sparkled with mischief as she wrapped Tilda in a tight embrace before withdrawing and taking in her appearance from head to stocking-covered toes. "You look breathtakingly innocent."

Edith noted a flash of unease when Tilda's soft, brown eyes widened.

Tilda, for all her bravado, was petrified.

Edith stepped forward and wrapped her arms around Tilda, much as Luci had a moment before, pushing from her mind the revelation that the girl's shoulders shook with nerves. "You are beautiful. You are smart. And today was a perfect way to start your married life. I only hope that Ophelia, Luci, and I are blessed with such generous husbands," Edith whispered to her friend.

"Thank you, Edith. You have always been a great friend." Tilda melted into Edith's embrace before pulling back. "I must hurry. It will not do for my *husband* to arrive and find I have fled. He said he would arrive by half past midnight, after attending to a few business matters."

Luci slipped her arm through Tilda's, while Ophelia grabbed the book she'd been reading and held it to her chest as she followed the women toward the door.

"Now remember that thing we spoke about. That thing with your tong…" Luci's whispers trailed off when the women moved out of hearing.

"I will extinguish the candles," Edith called to their retreating backs.

"Always the responsible one," Luci said over her shoulder with a smirk.

Ophelia paused at the threshold, her long, auburn locks mussed as usual. "I will help you."

"No, hurry along," Edith said, waving the woman off. "I know you are eager to return to your book. It will take but a few moments. I will meet you in our room as soon as I am done."

"If you insist." Ophelia smiled. With the corridor light at her back, she appeared an angel with her tousled hair and pale complexion. "I am eager to see how the fair Lady Daniella escapes the rogue pirate, Xavier."

Edith laughed softly. "Well, do get back to their story."

The woman didn't wait a moment longer, she flipped her book open and began reading as she turned to follow Tilda and Luci through the door.

Edith hurried about the room with the candlesnuffer, and before long, the salon was cast in shadows. The only remaining light came from a single lit candle—and the sconce in the hallway.

Grabbing the candleholder, Edith made certain that

the room was as they'd found it—tidy, without a thing out of place—and turned to pull the door closed behind her, her friends nowhere in sight.

A scream tore apart the stillness of the sleeping manor, echoing down every hallway and bouncing off closed doors.

The hair on the back of Edith's neck stood on end, and goose pimples spread across her bare arms as the shriek cut off, followed by the *thump, thump, thump* of something.

"Edith!" Lucianna shouted. "Ophelia!"

With her empty hand, Edith took hold of her skirts and ran toward the foyer, unconcerned that candle wax splattered on her exposed hand and the floor in her rush.

Edith turned the corner…and halted dead in her tracks, her heart pounding clear out of her chest.

A sob escaped Ophelia as her book slipped from her grasp and hit the polished floor.

Edith took a few steps until she stood at Ophelia's side. Luci was crouched on the bottom landing of the stairs, her long, raven locks blocking Edith's view of what she knelt over.

"Luci." Edith took a step forward as her friend stood. "What is it—"

But there was no need to go on. A trail of soft brown hair lay across the bottom stair, spilling onto the foyer floor.

"No, no, no," Edith sobbed as she hurried forward. "This cannot be—"

"He did this." The venom in Luci's tone had Edith looking away from the prone body of Tilda to where Luci stood, pointing toward the top of the stairs.

Following her friend's indicated direction, Edith narrowed her eyes on the darkened landing above them but could make out nothing—no person, no movement, no noise.

"Who?" Ophelia squeaked behind her.

"That is not important at this moment," Edith scolded, hurrying to Tilda's side. "We must wake her up, make sure she is all right and call for the duke—and a physician."

"There is no point." Luci knelt next to Edith, sweeping Tilda's hair from her face. "She is gone."

Vacant, chestnut-brown eyes stared back at her.

Tilda's doe eyes, always seeing to the heart of a matter, were empty of life. Tilda's carefree demeanor and the positive outlook she so desperately adored would never guide Edith again. Never again would Edith and her wonderful friend giggle behind their fans at some London dandy, cloaked in all the colors of a peacock's feathers, nor amble in the park, speaking of matters much more delicate—their fears, their passions, and their hopes for the future.

In the blink of an eye, it was all gone; as if the last sixteen years of friendship had never been.

A candle extinguished at the end of a long day.

"They argued," Luci insisted, grasping Edith's arm to halt her from touching Tilda. "He was up there, and he pushed her. I swear it."

Edith was helpless to take her eyes off Tilda, still unmoving at the bottom of the stairs. Even if her eyes hadn't been open, staring at the chandelier above, Edith would have known something was not right. Tilda's head was cocked at an odd angle, and one arm was tucked behind her back under her prone frame. Her demure, white nightshift was tangled between her legs, exposing her stocking-clad calves.

Tilda's innocent yet intense light was gone. It did not fade over time as it should, but was cast out without warning.

"Wha-wha-what should we do?" Ophelia wailed.

"We will rouse the house and tell them what the duke has done!" Lucianna shot to her feet once more. "Someone must have heard the commotion."

Edith glanced around the foyer, deserted except for

Luci, Ophelia, Edith, and, of course, Tilda. "You are correct. I heard her scream, and then the thump"—Edith cringed at her choice of word—"as she fell down."

"She did *not* fall." Lucianna's tone reached hysterics as she narrowed her glare on Edith. "She was *pushe*d by Abercorn!"

The trio stood, staring at one another. Tears overflowed and fell down Ophelia's reddened face, while Luci appeared far more in control. Her widened green eyes held no hint of the waterworks Ophelia had been reduced to. Edith was oddly in between—neither overtaken by grief nor completely in command of her faculties. Edith reached out toward Luci, but the woman ignored her hand.

"How could this happen?" Ophelia asked, stooping to collect her book as she dashed the tears away.

Luci's long, onyx hair swung over her shoulder as she turned to Ophelia. "That is a question for him. You saw him, right, Ophelia?"

The color drained from the girl's face, making her pale complexion turn almost green.

"Tell her what you saw." Luci took an intimidating step toward Ophelia. "You were standing right here."

"I—I—I was reading." Ophelia turned to Edith, her book held tightly against her bosom. "I swear it, Edith, I did not see anything. I was reading about Xavier and—"

"What is going on here?" Townsend, the Abercorn butler, bustled into the foyer, his hair askew as if the noise had pulled him from slumber. "Your Grace!" His eyes widened and fastened on Tilda as he rushed across the room to where she lay. His hand moved to her wrist and settled. "No pulse. She has no pulse!"

The servant shuffled to his feet, teetering for a moment at the shock of seeing his new mistress dead at the bottom of the grand staircase—on her wedding night.

"Petunia, Petunia!" Townsend shouted as he flapped his arms to and fro, rushing toward the kitchens. "Petunia! We must summon His Grace. Petunia, where in all that is holy are you, woman?"

Doors opened, and voices sounded above from the guests' wing as Townsend continued calling for Petunia.

Edith hadn't the faintest notion whom Petunia was, but she was obviously very important.

"Oh, Your Grace!" Townsend said, staring toward the top of the stairs. "Please, do not look. This is not for your eyes."

Scanning the landing above, Edith noted the duke, still garbed in his wedding day finery, his once blond hair now shot through with grey, starting down the stairs with a tumbler in hand. His leisurely pace and unhurried movements spoke volumes. Either he'd had no hand in the matter of Tilda's fall, or he knew damn well what had happened and could care less. He took a measured swallow from his tumbler, and his eyes narrowed as he scrutinized the scene below.

Abercorn had not yet set eyes upon his bride—lying prone below him, a trickle of blood now escaping her parted lips.

Or perhaps he knew exactly how Tilda lay, haphazardly broken. From the stiff set of his shoulders and his cold, unaffected stare toward the gathering in his foyer, Edith did not know.

Out of the corner of her eye, Edith watched Luci's hands ball into fists at her sides, and her face redden in fury.

Could the duke have pushed his new bride down the stairs as Lucianna claimed? If so, what did he gain by doing so? The thought that a wealthy lord, with everything within his grasp, would take a young, beautiful woman as his bride only to push her to her death before the marriage had even been consummated made absolutely no sense.

And how could the man look so unaffected by it

all?

CHAPTER 1

It is hereby stated that this writer has born firsthand witness to the 7th Duke of Montrose, scandalously alone with a golden-haired nymph in his private opera box, all whilst betrothed to the widow, Lady Cavendish.

As this writer can also attest, Lady Cavendish's hair is pure night, compared to the observed doxy's crown of light. Let this article stand as proof that Lady Cavendish would do well to find herself another eligible lord to take as husband.

-Mayfair Confidential, London Daily Gazette

St. James Place, London
January 1815

TRISTON NEVILLE, VISCOUNT Torrington, glared at his father, forcing himself to breathe in deeply and hold the stale air, heavy with cigar smoke, in his lungs to avoid it exiting in a rush of rage.

The Marquis of Downshire couldn't possibly fathom what he was asking of his son. Triston doubted his father understood the ludicrous nature of his demands, masked as simple fatherly requests.

"Did you hear me, Triston?" His father's nostrils flared, and the tiny vein that ran up his forehead pulsed…once, twice, three times. The man's frown deepened, and Triston was uncertain if the marquis was annoyed at his son's antics or only mildly agitated.

To be fair, Triston had been aiming for annoyance.

He straightened his shoulders, holding in his sigh once again, but responded before his father fainted from holding his breath. "Yes, Father. I heard you and will keep all you've said in mind."

"You will accompany your sisters during their Season?"

"Yes."

"You will endeavor to not draw attention to yourself and, therefore, away from your sisters?"

Triston looked up at the study ceiling, attempting to suppress his irritation. "I have never sought the *ton*'s notice, if you will remember."

Downshire stood, pushing his chair back. He placed his hand flat upon the desk separating the men and leaned forward. "That is neither here nor there."

In his younger days, Triston would have needed to steel himself from quaking in terror at his father's imposing stance and razor-edged words. However, those days passed when Triston grew several inches taller than the marquis, and his shoulders spread far wider than his sire's. Though both men towered over six feet in height and had matching golden-brown hair, Triston was larger on every scale that mattered— including intellect, which he hadn't vocalized since leaving the schoolroom for Eton.

"Father, I will do my best to make certain Lady Dow—" A movement over his father's shoulder, out the study window, caught Triston's notice. A flash of white was visible in the tree between the Downshire townhouse and their neighbor's. "I will make sure Esmee is not inconvenienced in any way."

Normally, his stepmother's name would have stuck in his throat, clawing to get free as he attempted to keep it unsaid. At present, he was determined not to allow the woman to overshadow his day; it was enough Triston would be forced to accompany the dreadful woman on social outings whenever she chose to attend.

His father nodded, apparently accepting Triston's pledge to see his sisters, Prudence and Chastity, safely wed before the year was out. To do that, the girls needed proper gowns with all the trimmings, and then needs must be presented to society to have the opportunity to meet eligible lords—all without their raven-haired stepmother criticizing their every move.

Triston leaned forward slightly to gain a better view out his father's study window. There was certainly something going on; however, alerting the marquis to it would not be wise and only lengthen their meeting. Blond hair hung down the back of a petite, female frame, the flash of her white petticoats being what had drawn his attention in the first place.

"Very well, Triston, I believe..." His father's brow scrunched, his eyes narrowing on his only son. "Are you even listening to me?"

"Of course." Triston took his eyes on the figure nestled in the tree. "It is only I have a prior engagement I am tardy for."

"A prior engagement, you say?" the marquis asked. His father's face reddened once more when Triston nodded. "You knew full well we meet each week at this precise time and place."

"Unfortunately, this could not be avoided." Triston shook his head as if he were loath to depart his father's home. "I surely must take my leave."

"If you must—"

Triston didn't wait for him to finish before turning and stalking toward the open study door.

His father's words echoed in his wake. "Impertinent, always were and always will be. Shut my door!"

Triston pulled the door closed, the thud reverberating through his entire body, though in a satisfying way.

He'd bought himself another week. Seven full days until he would be summoned again to his father's study to discuss trivial matters to keep up the appearance that the men were not at extreme odds with one another.

Triston only hoped that society had bought the ruse they'd been carrying on with since the marquis married his third and latest wife. If not, the *ton* would take great exception to his return to society, even with his two young sisters on his arms.

The hall window afforded a view similar to the study.

Triston took the few steps necessary and stood framed in the arched panes, gazing out as the afternoon sun warmed him through the glass. Sure enough, there was a woman perched in a Downshire tree, hunched over and staring at Lord Abercorn's upper window. A thick limb prodding her back prevented her from sitting completely upright.

It appeared his father requesting he accompany his sisters during their debut Season was only one of the peculiar occurrences he would witness during his day. Triston was hard-pressed to determine which was more alarming: his need to return to society, or a woman perched precariously in a plum tree.

Certainly, one did not regularly see a person, a woman especially, balanced on a thin tree limb at least six feet off the ground.

He tapped the window to gain her attention.

No response.

Triston looked up at the window she stared at, but the sun only reflected a glare off the glass, preventing him from seeing what held her attention.

Turning his focus toward the front drive and then back toward the gardens, Triston searched for the Downshire's groundskeeper. Frederick was usually tending the roses lining the drive during Triston's weekly visits to his father's home, but today he seemed to be absent.

He watched as the woman slipped something into her skirts, rubbing her hands together and looking about.

Was she not concerned someone would question why she was in a tree?

Triston shook his head. If the groundskeeper were nowhere in sight, it was his responsibility to inquire as to why the woman was trespassing on Downshire property.

That and assist her down from her perilous post.

LADY EDITH PELTON sat perched in a tree, her head bent low, and a branch poking into her backside. She was filthy, she was sore, and she hadn't managed to learn anything from the last several hours. The only thing she'd witnessed was the duke moving from his office on the first floor to the second floor—after a particularly buxom woman with midnight locks had joined him. They hadn't entered any of the rooms facing her direction, nor had they returned below. That had been nearly an hour ago, and Edith had yet to note any other movement on the second floor, besides the occasional servant attending to their chores.

If she returned yet again with no new information on the Duke of Abercorn, nothing that condemned him for his wrongdoings—nor absolved him of his accused crimes—Lucianna would be irate. She'd likely demand to investigate the man herself, or worse yet, instruct Ophelia to write the article for the *Gazette*, attacking Abercorn, regardless of his culpability in Tilda's death.

Edith would not allow that to happen, could not permit her dear friend to ruin a man's life with no proof of his misconducts. Lucianna had agreed to wait until sufficient evidence existed, but with each passing day— and more articles submitted to the *Gazette*—her friend grew impatient.

Suddenly, a drapery on the second story toward the back of the townhouse was pulled aside, revealing a quite naked, raven-haired woman, her long tresses the only thing covering her exposed bosom.

It was impossible for Edith to take her eyes off the sight before her as the duke, fully clothed, stepped up behind the woman, wrapping his arms around her tightly as he fondled her breasts. The large window framed the couple perfectly. The woman began to sway before Abercorn, her backside still flush with his front.

Edith's face flamed red with embarrassment at the scandalous spectacle.

The duke whipped the woman around until her naked breasts were pressed against his chest, and the woman's rounded derriere pressed solidly against the windowpane. Abercorn slowly moved his lips to the woman's neck and traced his mouth along her shoulder before suddenly straightening and throwing his head back in a silent chuckle.

She wondered what the raven-haired beauty had said to gain such a reaction from the cold, stoic duke.

Edith's stare narrowed on the pair as the woman reached up and began to undo Abercorn's cravat.

Before Edith even suspected what was happening, the duke's eyes scanned the landscape outside his townhouse, his glare seeming to find Edith perched in the tree bordering his property. Abruptly, Edith ducked her head and slipped her journal into the secret pocket she'd sewn into each of her gowns for exactly this purpose before easing from the branch she sat on to scurry down the tree.

I cannot be caught, I cannot be caught, I cannot be caught, she chanted, placing her booted feet on another branch before dipping low to take hold of it and swing down to the ground below.

Almost there. Edith's hands were mere inches from grasping the thick limb to lower herself…only six feet from escape.

"You, there!" a deep voice sounded behind her. "What are you doing up there?"

"Eeep!" The sudden exclamation took her mind off the limb she reached for, and Edith's boot caught on her skirt, causing her to miss the branch completely. She stiffened her body as she fell, bracing for the impact she knew was to come as the air rushed by her.

The seconds slowed.

Giving her ample time to contemplate what she'd done in her life to end up falling from a tree in the fashionable St. James area of London, her arms pinwheeling as she hoped to ease her landing.

Thump.

Everything went dark, and Edith feared she'd landed on her head, doing irreparable damage.

She blinked several times and willed her mind to command her fingers to wiggle and her toes to curl in her boots.

Everything worked.

She said a silent prayer to whoever was looking out for her.

"I asked what you are doing on my property!" the man huffed.

Edith blinked again—still complete darkness. Maybe she *had* hit her head on the way down, but would it not ache?

"Do stop this ridiculousness and remove your garments from your head."

She moved silently, rolling to her side, a resounding pain in her backside cluing her in to exactly how she'd landed.

Lifting her hands, Edith pushed at whatever covered her sight, only to see a pair of Hessians solidly placed beside her. Lowering the material farther, she noted thick, muscular calves leading to tree trunk-sized thighs clad in tightly tailored breeches.

Edith cringed, allowing the material to fall back

into place, blocking out all view of the man once more.

"I would suggest righting your skirts, as your derriere is exposed to all and sundry who happen to pass by on the street," the man commanded sternly.

From the dampness seeping from the ground beneath her hip and into her exposed knickers, Edith suspected she'd landed in a particularly well-tended and watered part of foliage.

The mention of her derriere brought back images of the raven-haired beauty's bare buttocks pressed firmly to the window of Abercorn's townhouse. Her face heated immediately, and Edith longed for nothing more than to stay hidden.

She wished a carriage would come along and put her out of her misery, as it were.

It was difficult to decide which was more embarrassing: her fall from the tree, her skirts being cast over her head, or that whoever the man standing above her was had witnessed it all.

"If I remain as such, will you go away and act as if this never happened?" Edith asked.

"What sort of gentleman would I be if I did not verify a damsel in distress was uninjured after a fall such as this?" His Hessians crunched dry, fallen leaves as he moved before her. "Besides, you are still trespassing, and I cannot allow that to go unresolved."

Suddenly, her skirts were pulled away, and Edith looked up, the bright sun momentarily blinding her, causing spots of colors to cross her vision. She closed her eyes tightly and rubbed at her face.

"I am going nowhere, so it's best if you remove your hands from your face and permit me to help you regain your feet."

"What if I simply roll myself into the street and allow the next carriage or man on horseback to resolve this dilemma for us?" she said into the palms of her gloved hands.

"I would say that is a mess I would not relish

cleaning up." His stern tone had lessened, taking on an almost jovial quality.

Edith allowed her hands to fall from her face, and the man's outstretched hand appeared before her. She took a moment to ponder his offer, knowing if she raised her eyes to his, she'd be far more exposed than her backside had been only a moment before.

"Come now, I do not bite—unless commanded to," he said with a chuckle.

She couldn't avoid the man any longer. He was not going away, nor did he appear the type to allow questions to go unanswered.

But blast it all, Edith did not need to accept his assistance to gain her footing.

Her backside and pride were already bruised; she had no intentions of accepting his hand.

With a huff, Edith placed her gloved palms upon the dirt on either side of her, preparing to push herself to her feet—without his help.

But with the action, her gaze traveled from the man's offered hand and back to his thick thighs. The male could be a Highlander of old with such a foundation. Edith was helpless to stop her eyes from straying farther upward. His muscular legs gave way to a solid midsection that had her halting at his expansive chest. She need not allow her mind to wander far to know that under his linen shirt lay a chest of pure muscle, capped off by broad, sinewy shoulders certainly capable of lifting a fallen tree. Or a damsel in distress, as he'd dubbed her.

Edith swallowed, gulping down her purr of pleasure. What had overtaken her? He was only a man—a very *strong* man, his frame proving he exerted himself vigorously with regularity. It would not surprise her if he spent each day undertaking pursuits of manual labor, carrying carriage wheels as if they weighed no more than a bowl of orange marmalade.

He cleared his throat. "It is improper to stare,

miss."

Edith's eyes widened in alarm. She *was* staring, and with no sense of regret. Whatever had come over her?

The moment she pushed on her palms to try and raise herself, a shot of pain traveled to her elbow. "Mayhap it is more than my backside that is bruised," she mumbled.

"I am here to assist," he repeated.

"You would like that much, I am certain, Lord—" Edith's words ended abruptly. She hadn't any notion if the man before her *was* a lord. He could be no more than a common gentleman. "I can stand without help, but thank you nonetheless."

"Torrington."

"Pardon?" Her eyes snapped to his face—another colossal mistake as her mouth gaped at the Adonis before her, the noonday sun highlighting his umber brown hair, chiseled jawline, and decidedly aristocratic nose. He was what the great poets of old wrote about in their sonnets. He was the image every artist struggled to achieve in oils. He was what sculptors in Roman times worked a lifetime to create.

And he was standing before her...flesh and blood.

His eyes seemingly capable of seeing to her very soul.

"My name, miss. Lord Torrington—Triston if you prefer, as I feel we are now adequately acquainted." He smirked at his jest and shook his hand before her face once more.

"Lord Torrington, it is," Edith said, relenting and taking his hand.

"Come, miss, we can do away with formalities. After all, I know the fabric of your knickers." His arrogant, amused grin grew, softening the hard line of his jaw—if it were possible.

At her gasp, he chuckled, hoisting her to her feet with one swift tug of her arm.

CHAPTER 2

WHEN SHE'D REGAINED her feet, the golden-haired siren pulled her hand from Triston's quickly, as if his touch had scorched her palm through her sullied glove.

He raised a brow in question.

As a gentleman, he should inquire as to any injuries obtained in her fall. Yet, the memory of the sight of her pristine linen drawers, her skirts and cloak flung haphazardly over her head, took up his every available thought, making it impossible to organize his words in any semblance of order.

Her copper-colored eyes widened on him and then narrowed.

"How dare you—" she stammered.

"How dare I?" He took a step closer, causing her to stumble back. "It is you whom I found lurking in a tree—on the property of a home where you do not belong."

Triston did his best to keep his tone stern and his stance intimidating, though the urge to laugh nearly overtook him. Truly, he didn't care what the woman was doing in the tree. However, he would be lying to himself if he didn't admit that her motives intrigued him, especially as it took his mind off his *meeting* with his sire, the Marquis of Downshire.

It was more of a summons than an optional invitation to meet with his father to discuss the upcoming Season and his younger sisters' presentation to the *ton*.

Yes, Triston would much rather focus his mind…and imagination as it were, on the jumbled woman before him.

Her brow scrunched, and her lips pressed together. "How do you assume to know if I belong here or not, my lord?" Her hands landed on her hips, her tone challenging.

"I assure you, I would know if you belonged on Downshire property." He crossed his arms, refusing to advance any farther but also unwilling to back down. He'd had quite enough of women thinking they could order him about and instruct him on what is what. He was a bloody viscount, after all, heir to a marquis. The slip of a woman before him hadn't any notion whom she dealt with.

Instead of holding her tongue, however, the hellion laughed—at him. A sweet, melodic sound that echoed down the row of townhouses along St. James.

"What, may I inquire, is so comical?" Triston demanded.

She sobered enough to reply, "You, thinking you know where I do and do not belong—or even whose property we are standing upon."

Maybe he should have thought twice before approaching the woman. She seemed a bit peculiar, to say the least—and possibly utterly insane at worst. And this was exactly the type of situation his father demanded he refrain from being involved in until after Prudence and Chastity were safely, legally, and indisputably betrothed.

Yet, could an angel of such captivating beauty be absolutely unhinged?

It would be the ultimate paradox.

However, it would be little different from his own dear sisters, Pru and Chastity, who were also a complete contradiction. They were not beauties, but their wit, grace, and agreeableness would make them the perfect brides for any man—if one could only look past their plain, wallflowerish exteriors.

"Why are you looking at me as though I've sprouted horns and will gallop away at any moment?" she asked.

"I was contemplating the possibility that you are stark raving mad." Honesty was good—forthright responses were always what Triston fell back on when confronted with a question he'd rather not answer.

"Why, I never..." She jammed her gloved hands into her pockets as her voice faltered, her face a perfectly   composed   mask   of   rage. "That...well...certainly..."

Her angry expression told Triston this was another occurrence his father was determined to avoid during the upcoming Season. A public confrontation between his wife and son would draw unwelcome attention to them all, casting Pru and Chastity in a negative light.

Her shoulders straightened, and her chin notched up several degrees. "I assure you I am not mad—neither insane nor angry."

He would beg to differ as she'd just been caught perched in a tree, then had fallen from said tree—which was irrefutable even to those who hadn't seen, as she had leaves stuck to her cloak and a stick protruding from her hair. "I am pleased to hear this, but you still have not told me what you are doing on my property, nor your name."

She glanced over her shoulder and up at Lord Abercorn's townhouse before turning back to him. "There really is no need for all of this. I am uninjured, as you can see." To prove her point, she flapped her arms, shrugged her shoulders, and bent over, touching her toes before straightening with a confident smile.

A lock of pure-spun golden hair came loose from her updo and fell across her face, the stick coming with it.

Unaware of his intentions, Triston reached out and pulled the stick free, then presented it to her before tossing it into a nearby shrub.

"Thank you, my lord." She pushed the wayward lock of hair from her face. "I will be going now."

"How will you arrive home?" He looked up and down St. James. No waiting carriage and no horse were in sight—besides his stallion, Blitz, being led around from his father's stables. "I cannot, in good conscience, allow you to leave unchaperoned without proper conveyance."

Her eyes darted down the drive bordering the foliage where they stood when she heard his stallion's hooves on the cobblestone.

"Not so fast." Triston made to grab her arm before she fled, but the woman flinched, freezing to her spot as if too terrified to move. "I only seek your name and the reason for you being on my property. That is all."

"I am not on your property, and you have no right to demand my name."

THE MAN WAS swiftly turning from an Adonis to Dolon—demanding, arrogant, and forthright. She much preferred admiring him when he kept his mouth closed. Edith hadn't thought her schooling in Greek and Roman mythology would ever be of use, yet, here she was, dredging from memory the attributes of legends long past.

Lord Torrington, or whatever the man claimed his name to be, was incorrigible. Unlike any gentleman she'd ever met.

Not to touch on the matter of his handsomeness…which did not matter to Edith in the slightest, yet was undeniable.

"My name is none of your concern because I am not, in fact, on your property." There, she'd spoken her mind—and the world hadn't crumbled around her, nor had the Adonis before her disappeared into the mist. "And I would thank you not to concern yourself with my travel arrangements."

"Whose property do you assume we are standing on?" His brow rose, and the corner of his lip turned up in a smirk.

"Lord Abercorn's," she stated simply.

Torrington pointed to a line of stones, barely noticeable but still a definite line between her and the Abercorn townhouse property. "As you can see, the tree you climbed is securely on Downshire property. And I have every right to demand your reason for being on the marquis' land—and more to the fact, summon the magistrate."

She'd assumed being caught by Abercorn, or the woman he currently shared his chambers with, was as dire as her afternoon could get. Yet, the lord before her seemed determined to have the information he sought. But what would he do with it? If he took her name to Abercorn, she and her friends could be in serious peril; and if he insisted on calling the authorities, her parents would be notified.

Edith would not allow that to happen. "Wait a moment, did you not say your name is Torrington?"

"I did," he confirmed with a nod.

"And we stand on the Marquis of Downshire's property?"

"Correct once more." He said the words slowly as if she were daft.

Yet, it was Edith's turn to smirk. "Well, as I see it, you have no authority here if you are not the marquis." Maybe, just maybe, she'd be able to escape without Abercorn or her parents finding out. It would only leave her to inform Luci and Ophelia they were no closer to proving Lord Abercorn's culpability in Tilda's death.

The positive side was that she would be free to continue searching for evidence that Abercorn had pushed his new bride down the stairs of his country manor on the night of his wedding.

Edith slipped her hand into her pocket to make sure her journal hadn't fallen from its place. When her fingers touched the familiar leather binding, Edith's assuredness returned, and she pivoted to depart.

"Where are you going?" The lord's feet sounded behind her as she picked her way through the shrubs on her way to the street. "Stop."

Edith glanced over her shoulder, determined to keep out of Lord Torrington's reach until she made it to Pall Mall and the nearest hackney she could wave down. "Good day, my lord."

CHAPTER 3

TRISTON GLANCED ABOUT the crowded ballroom, or at least as much of the room as he could see from his current location. "Do we plan to hide behind these potted palms all evening?"

His question gained him a scathing look from his two sisters, six and seven years his junior, before they turned their stares back to the ballroom in unison.

"For at least another set," Pru hissed, her pastel green gown blending in exquisitely with the foliage bordering the dance floor. He wished he could say the dress complimented her just as exquisitely, except the shade clashed with her pale complexion, and the gown was far too tight by any person's standards. "Now hush, or we will be noticed."

"We are at a ball, Prudence, we are supposed to be seen." He shook his head at this sister's reprimand.

"We are not ready to be seen as yet, brother," Chastity chimed in, her dull brown curls bouncing as she shook her head. "If we are discovered, that will mean we must speak with someone."

"Which we are certainly not ready to do."

The pair shared an exasperated look, leading Triston to think that something was going on he was not privy to, which would not surprise him.

It was going to be a long Season if this was how it was to start. Triston glanced at his sisters on either side of him. Many mistook the pair for twins, though they were born ten months apart. Their hair was always styled in a similar fashion, their gowns always the same cut, and they rarely left one another's side.

A pang of jealousy hit him, something he'd endured far more often in his younger days. Not that he was ancient, by any means, but at twenty and three, Triston was securely the older, odd-man-out sibling. Certainly, he adored his sisters, doted on them even, but they shared a bond that Triston could never hope to be a part of.

"I know I am going to regret inquiring, but *why* are you not ready to do that?" he asked, as the musicians concluded another set, and the dancers departed the floor.

"Because, dear brother…" Chastity spoke slowly, as if uncertain he understood her words. "If we are noticed, that would mean we need speak with someone, likely a horde of eligible men seeking a dance partner, and we are not ready for such a commitment."

"And because, dear brother," Pru said, picking up when Chastity sighed, "we have many things we seek to see before becoming entangled with a gentleman who might offer for our hands."

Both girls' heads bobbed, but they did not take their eyes off the dance floor when the musicians signaled another set was about to start.

Triston couldn't help his open-mouthed stare. Commitment? Eligible men? And offers of marriage? He wondered if his sisters had a looking glass in their bedchamber—or if their eyesight was good enough to afford them an adequate view of the other women in the room.

Not that his sisters would not find suitable matches, maybe even highly sought after lords with the dowries his father had settled on each girl; however, they were not diamonds of the first water. They took much more after their father and Triston than their mother. Both debutantes more firmly weighted on the side of stout rather than lithe. They were built in a similar fashion to Triston: broad of shoulder and thick of waist, with legs more suitably constructed for scaling tall mountains than graceful waltzes.

For a man, the attributes were looked upon favorably by the fairer sex.

While for women, men usually gazed upon his sisters as if they were reckoning the value of a brood mare.

Which only made Triston seek to put his fist through the unlucky bastards' faces.

They were his baby sisters, after all—they were delicate *bloody* flowers.

Innocent, intelligent, and great conversationalists.

And any man who sought one of their hands in marriage—or even a dance—should best well understand that.

This was exactly the reason Triston had argued with his father a few days prior. He was not qualified to escort his siblings about London. It was not safe—for his sisters, himself, or any sorry gent who thought themselves worthy of one of the Downshire sisters.

Maybe Triston's doting ways had given the pair an incorrect estimation of their visual appeal, leaving him to tidy up the mess that would be made when they either hid behind these palms all Season or turned down every man who asked to put their name upon Pru's or Chastity's dance cards.

"I am in need of refreshments, ladies." Triston stepped around his sisters and turned, blocking their view of the room. "It would be best if the pair of you accompany me."

He held out both arms, and his sisters eyed his offer with matching skeptical expressions before slipping their arms through his.

"Very wise, dear sisters," Triston whispered. "I think you both are in need of a glass of sherry."

"Heavens no," they gasped in unison.

"Stepmother would never allow it," Chastity said.

"Yes, Lady Downshire is adamantly against women of fine breeding consuming any type of spirits," Prudence agreed, keeping true to her name.

"Well, the good Lady Downshire is not here to witness anything," Triston argued. "What she does not see will not hurt her, as the saying goes."

Pru's eyes widened. "But she will find out."

"She always finds out," Chastity said, her head shaking. "And then we will be made to do without."

Triston weaved through the crowd gathered around the edges of the ballroom, careful to not make eye contact with anyone, lest they approach him for conversation.

However, he could not disagree with his sisters' fears in regards to Esmee Neville, the latest Marchioness of Downshire. She was a spiteful woman with a tendency to enact retribution on anyone who disobeyed her commands. She was a raven-haired beauty, who captured a man's heart before crushing it between her elegant, pale hands; watching the pieces crumble to the ground before stepping on them.

Not that Triston could blame his father for falling in love with such a beautiful creature—he only wished the marquis would have heeded his son's warning about the sharpness of the woman's talons.

"Do not allow the beast to crush your spirits, my dear sisters." They stepped into the line for refreshments. "She will shortly attain what she wants, a babe of her own, and then she will leave the three of us to our own devices. I am certain of it."

The current marchioness was only a year younger than Triston and had yet to start her own family. But he assumed she would soon, as she did not consider the marquis' previous children up to her required standards, nor would her position be solidified if something were to happen to her husband without a child born of the union. And so, she'd set out to provide Downshire with a spare heir, should something untoward happen to Triston.

The girls looked to one another before Pru responded. "We will have one sherry—"

"Wonderful!"

"To split between us," Chastity finished. "And we shall endeavor to hurry to our rooms when we arrive home to avoid the marchioness catching the scent of spirits on our persons."

"Whatever you must do," Triston said with a chuckle. "I am happy I no longer have to put up with the ice queen's edicts."

Both girls pouted at his mention of no longer residing with them at their father's townhouse. "We do not understand why we could not go with you," Chastity whined.

"Yes, Esmee would not mind, so long as we were no longer underfoot."

Triston took in their downcast expressions and, not for the first time, he sensed they felt as if he'd abandoned them. "You both know living in a boarding house is not proper for two young women, especially ones seeking to find elevated matches."

"We are not looking to wed!" they protested as one.

He'd known the comment would distract them from thoughts of Triston's recent departure from their family home; however, he could not reside under his father's roof a moment longer, especially if it meant he remained under Esmee's control.

However, the girls' insistence that they were not looking to wed was preposterous. Every young debutante was taking part in the elaborate fiasco that was the Marriage Market for the eventual outcome of…marriage. He could not see Esmee taking kindly to

Pru and Chastity spending money on a Season when neither was actually inclined to wed.

As the marquis' third wife—Triston's mother having passed from influenza when he was only a toddler, and Pru and Chastity's mother having died giving birth to Chastity—the woman was set on vanquishing all memories of those who'd come before her, even Downshire's previous children.

And that meant marrying off Triston's two young sisters.

A voice cleared behind them, and both women stiffened on his arms, making no move to turn to see who sought their attention.

"Good evening, my lord." The deep, throaty voice sparked a familiar memory. "Lady Prudence, Lady Chastity. You are both the height of composure this evening."

Abercorn.

Their father's neighbor—and friend. And a man Triston was barely acquainted with beyond their two bordering townhomes. In fact, it was odd to have the blonde vixen mention Abercorn followed by the man appearing.

"Good evening, Your Grace," Triston greeted the elderly man as he turned. "Lovely to see you."

"And you, as well, Torrington." Abercorn's evening attire was tailored to fit his frame perfectly—and Triston suspected outfitting a man as tall and rail-thin as Abercorn was no easy feat. "Your father said you'd be in attendance tonight, and I must claim a dance from both Lady Prudence and Lady Chastity."

A shiver went through both of his sisters at the man's lecherous stare.

He wondered if his sisters knew things he did not.

How his father stood the company of the duke was beyond Triston's comprehension; however, Pru and Chastity dipped into graceful curtseys before holding out their wrists with their dance cards.

Abercorn hastily scribbled his name on Pru's card, but only glanced at Chastity's blank slip. "A set is about to begin. May I have this dance, Lady Chastity?"

Triston wanted to deny the gentleman's request, but was left without reason. The duke was his father's friend—and even if the girls despised the marchioness, they adored their father and always sought to please him, even if that meant dancing with a man old enough to be their father—or an uncle.

"Chastity would be honored," Triston answered when his sister's gloved hand squeezed his arm. He handed his sister off and watched as the pair made their way to the dance floor. "That man is an odd one."

Pru giggled, highly improperly, before ending it on a snort. "Chastity feels sorry for him."

"Sorry, why?"

She turned a stern look on him. "Dear brother, do you not follow societal gossip at all?"

"No." And he was surprised his sisters did. "Why in heavens name would I want to know what Lord so-and-so does after he deposits his wife following a ball? Or who the widow, Lady Palmer, has sunken her claws into this time." Mainly, his lack of interest was because he'd been the topic of hurtful, slanderous gossip, and he took zero stock in any of it.

Hell, his family was likely still a topic of conversation in most drawing rooms.

When a man's betrothed leaves him to marry his father, the *ton* does not forget.

Even now, Triston noticed a woman avert her stare when his eyes landed on her.

Yes, he was commissioned to see his sisters safely about London proper—not hoard all the attention for himself.

Thankfully, they'd reached the front of the refreshment line, and he selected two flutes of sherry. Handing one to Pru, Triston downed the other and held it out for a refill before they moved on.

"I hope you do not plan to slip deep into your cups this evening," Pru commented, her eyes wide with astonishment, her own glass forgotten in her hand.

He certainly would not disagree with a tumbler or two of scotch, but at best, he had watered-down sherry. "It would take an entire trough of this sherry to see even a hint of drunken behavior. Worry not, dear sister."

They resumed their place on the fringes of the dance floor and turned to watch Abercorn and Chastity swirl about with the other pairs—a bit slower than the other dancers, and less coordinated. Triston supposed age did that to a person.

His eyes settled on a trio of women standing on the far edge of the ballroom, across from Triston and Pru. The group also watched the duke and Chastity as they whirled in time to the beat.

An auburn-haired woman tried to hide her interest in the couple, while her two companions, a towering, midnight-haired beauty, and a woman with hair the color of spun gold, glared openly at Abercorn and Chastity. Triston could only gain a side profile of the group, but they were most definitely watching Chastity.

"Do you know those women?" he asked Pru, nodding in the group's direction.

Prudence took to her tiptoes to see over the dancing crowd. "Oh, yes. I do."

"Who are they?" Just then, the blonde woman turned in his direction, and his mind stopped short. It was the woman from outside his father's townhouse. Her hair was respectably coiffed, and her evening gown was expertly crafted to fit her short frame. He'd need ask after her seamstress, as she'd likely create a miracle for Pru and Chastity's wardrobe. "I do not think I have made their acquaintance."

Pru shook her head dejectedly. "It is unlikely you have. They were presented last Season, but quickly retreated after that unfortunate night."

"What unfortunate night?" he asked.

"And this is why you should take greater note of the gossip rags," Pru sighed. "They are Ladies Lucianna, Edith, and Ophelia. They were the talk of their Season, with their friend, Miss Tilda Guthton."

The last name was vaguely familiar; however, Triston was unsure from where he knew it. "What happened? Why would they retreat?"

Pru dropped his arm and turned to face him, bewilderment clouding her features. "How are you so unaware, Triston?" When he remained silent, she continued. "Miss Tilda became the Duchess of Abercorn only a few short weeks into last Season."

"Abercorn isn't wed," Triston challenged.

"He isn't wed *now*." Pru folded her arms across her chest and then quickly uncrossed them, running her hands down the front of her satin gown. "Miss Tilda…Lady Abercorn, died on the night of their wedding. Fell—or was pushed—down the main staircase, depending on who's account you believe."

Triston narrowed his eyes on the trio of women, suddenly making sense of why the blonde woman had perched herself in a Downshire tree to watch Abercorn's townhome. "And her friends believe she was pushed?"

Why in heaven's name would a duke take a wife only to see her gone on their wedding night? Besides, Triston found it hard to believe Abercorn capable of such an act.

"Mayhap." Pru shrugged and turned back toward the women. The dancers had moved, enabling his sister to gain a decent view across the dance floor. "The black-haired woman is stunning, is she not?"

Triston took his stare off the blonde to take in the sight of the tall, willowy, raven-haired beauty; however, his appeal for the darker variety of women had been snubbed long ago. Though it made sense for his sister to assume he would be taken with her.

"She is certainly alluring. What do you know of them and their families?" he asked in way of steering the conversation—hoping Pru didn't catch on to his true intentions.

"Lady Lucianna Constantine is the black-haired beauty. Lady Ophelia Fletcher is the one with the downcast eyes—a terrible introvert, they say. And the petite blonde woman is Lady Edith Pelton."

Lady Edith.

He allowed the name to roll about in his mind. He'd never heard of her before; which, from his sister's explanation, made ample sense. Triston had avoided society after his broken betrothal forced him into the unwanted spotlight of every gossip-minded matron in London. He glanced about the room at the mere thought, but found no one staring at him. It had taken two years, but finally, the scandal sheets had moved on to other topics of fodder.

"The trio only just arrived for the Season a few weeks ago, their mourning period having ended; however, it is said that not a single gentleman has dared ask them to dance or for a turn in the park." Pru lifted her chin as if she were impressed by the women's skill at keeping men at bay. "Chastity and I have been trying to gain an introduction since seeing them at the Crofton's garden party a fortnight ago, but the women do not often socialize, and quickly depart societal events after a brief appearance."

Most likely because the trio was spying on Abercorn.

Triston watched Lady Edith as she leaned close and whispered something to Lady Lucianna before nudging the auburn-haired chit to gain her attention, as well.

Their glares still intensely observed Abercorn's every movement. Did they wait for the man to strike again—in the middle of a crowded ballroom?

If Abercorn were able to get away with killing his

young bride, he would not be so foolish as to cause a scene before all of society.

Suddenly, Lady Edith's stare scanned the room—landing on him.

Prudence tugged at his arm and hissed, "They are watching us, brother. Mayhap they will talk to me."

The excitement in his sister's tone was evident; though Triston also sought to speak with the women, or more accurately, *one* of the women.

Lady Edith owed him answers, and Triston was determined to gain them, even if that meant confronting her in a crowded ballroom.

CHAPTER 4

EDITH SCRUTINIZED LORD Torrington across the crowded ballroom as the Duke of Abercorn returned his dance partner to the viscount's left side before taking the gloved hand of the woman on Torrington's right and returning to the dance floor.

The women held a striking resemblance to Torrington and must be a close relation—sisters, perhaps?

That would make the young women neighbors of Abercorn's—and likely friends. The woman now in the duke's arms seemed a bit too stiff and only spoke in answer to Abercorn's unheard words. She did not look the blushing debutante, thrilled to be dancing with a wealthy, eligible lord.

But, Torrington and the young women were positively acquainted with the duke. How close their relationship was, Edith could not guess.

However, she was vastly relieved she'd fled when she did, or Abercorn would have been informed of her presence outside his townhouse. If the neighbors were known to one another well enough to associate at a ball, then there was little doubt Torrington might share news of Edith's presence outside the Abercorn townhouse.

"Do you know the man?" Ophelia asked, leaning

close but managing to keep her eyes trained on the polished floor nonetheless.

The woman was perceptive, always had been, noting things that both Edith and Luci continually missed.

"Yes." Edith needed to distract her friends before other guests noticed the way the trio kept a close watch on Abercorn. "He caught me outside Abercorn's townhouse a few days ago."

"The day you fell out of the tree and bruised your backside?" Luci asked with a throaty chuckle, never taking her attention off Torrington. "He is certainly a handsome—"

Edith crossed her arms and cut Luci short. "That is him—all arrogant, incorrigible, and…"

"Massive," Ophelia sighed, her eyes moving from the floor to the hulking man across the room. "He looks as if he could drive a hansom cab…without the horses."

Edith took in Torrington's sheer size. His shoulders appeared far broader in a crowded ballroom, and his tight pants gave an optimal view of his muscular legs.

"It is likely the man must turn sideways to enter a door," Luci continued, prolonging the jest. "Those thighs could crush a boulder—imagine the fate of a woman between them."

"Lucianna," Ophelia hissed, her cheeks flaming with embarrassment as she glanced to both sides to make certain no one had heard what was spoken. "That is a highly improper topic for a ballroom."

"Yes, however, it does appease my imagination," Luci retorted with a sniff. "Do not be such a prude."

"I…well…I most certainly am not—"

"Did your mind instantly visualize the man, complete with bridle and reins, sans a stitch of clothing, pulling a hackney?" At Luci's question, Ophelia's eyes widened and quickly returned to the floor. "I thought not. Prude."

Edith cocked her head and examined Torrington once more. Her mind hadn't conjured Luci's visual either, but now she thought of little else. She averted her stare to stop her own flush and scanned the ballroom. Highlighted in shades of gold and blue sheer bolt fabrics, the chandeliers above cast a glow that sparkled off the polished silver pots holding tall palms in several spots around the room. Gentlemen and fashionably adorned ladies swirled about the dance floor while many wandered the room and out onto the terrace beyond.

She'd spotted Lord Torrington as he stood close to the refreshment table as the Duke of Abercorn had made his way toward them.

Where he'd come from, Edith didn't know. One moment, she and her friends were keeping watch on Abercorn's movements while avoiding any gentlemen who might ask one of them to dance; and the next, Lord Torrington stood with two demurely gowned brunettes on his arms. Not that she and her friends had been observing anyone but the duke; however, Edith had been shocked to see Torrington.

The man who currently observed her and her friends, just as they watched him.

"What is his name?" Luci purred, not verbalizing the one thing Edith heard loud and clear from her tone: what is the *handsome man's* name?

"Torrington. Lord Torrington." Edith watched him chuckle at something the woman on his arm said as he avoided eye contact with Edith. Pain shot through her jaw when she realized she clenched it tightly, her teeth grinding into one another. "He is certainly hiding something."

"Oh, I'd much enjoy seeing what his trousers are hiding." Luci's jest had Ophelia choking on her breath.

Irritation caused Edith's muscles to tense before she shrugged half-heartedly. "Likely nothing but an enlarged ego and unveiled arrogance."

"Why are you so overly critical of him?" Ophelia

asked. "Has he done something to displease you?"

"I would think his mere association with Abercorn should displease us all," Edith retorted. "I will admit the man is hiding something."

"Hiding something more elaborate than Abercorn?" Luci asked, intrigued.

"Possibly." Or Lord Torrington was nothing more than a lord born and bred to be the arrogant gentleman. He appeared the Goliath rather than the Adonis from their previous meeting. "I think it best I keep watch on him. If he is hiding something, I will find it—and Ophelia will use the information in her next *Mayfair Confidential* piece."

"Are you suggesting we stop our surveillance of Abercorn?" Lucianna set her long, gracefully gloved hands on her hips.

"You know we cannot jeopardize our true intentions and plans by reporting on Abercorn until we have solid proof of his culpability in Tilda's death," Edith argued, keeping her voice low. "If we write about him too soon, everyone in London will know who is behind the *Mayfair Confidential* articles in the *Gazette*."

Luci's eyes flared with anger. "Are you saying I did not see what I have told you I saw?"

"Come now, Lucianna," Ophelia soothed. "You know *we* believe you, but that accomplishes nothing if we cannot prove anything to the magistrate or Tilda's parents."

But Edith was uncertain she believed Luci's accounting from the night Tilda fell to her death. She wanted nothing more than to believe her friend and prove her accusation true, but until that happened, she refused to be party to a story that would ruin a man's life—more than they'd already ruined him.

They'd agreed to have Ophelia write a story on Abercorn only when they had irrefutable evidence and did not fear any backlash if they were discovered as the people behind the *Mayfair Confidential* pieces. But they were all in agreement on the importance of warning other debutantes against men with unsavory pasts, the tendency to drink heavily, or an inclination toward violence. So, each week on Thursday, the *London Daily Gazette* published a column called *Mayfair Confidential* that highlighted gentlemen with distasteful habits. As of now, no one suspected who was responsible for the pieces—but the instant Abercorn was mentioned, with Luci's firsthand account of the incident, there would be no doubt as to whom was supplying the information.

Edith was uncertain she was prepared for the repercussions once London—and the many men they worked to expose—knew they were responsible.

"Do not look now, Edith, but he is looking this way, and he does not appear happy to see you," Lucianna said with a laugh. For reasons unknown to Edith, Luci always acted untouchable and invincible, as if no person could harm her; however, the stark reality of the matter was they were all as susceptible to injury as Tilda had been. And they all knew where their dear friend was now after her hasty betrothal and marriage to a man over twice her age.

Edith notched her chin high and turned her narrowed stare in Torrington's direction. If the man thought to intimidate her, he vastly underestimated the woman he was dealing with.

CHAPTER 5

"TRISTON!" A VENOM-DIPPED voice, which many mistook for a honey-coated melody, called to him as he attempted to escape his father's townhouse without being waylaid after their weekly meeting. "Torry, stop, I am calling you."

He despised the pet name—always had—which was likely why his latest stepmother, Esmee, insisted on using it. The mere sound of her voice, and her quick steps behind him, had Triston longing to flee and never return.

His teeth clenched tight, and his jaw ached.

However, he knew enough to know that if he angered the woman by ignoring her and departing, she'd only take her wrath out on Pru and Chastity. Again, something he had little control over, and it irked him to no end.

"Yes, Esmee?" Triston pulled his lips into a smile, but judging from the way the woman shrank back in horror, it was more of a snarl. "What can I assist you with today?"

Meaning: in what way could she complicate his life?

She hurried down the hall after him and flipped her fan, connecting with his elbow. "You know I prefer you to call me Mother," she scolded. At his continued frown, she said, "But that is not why I stopped you. Your sisters and I are in need of your accompaniment to Hyde Park today."

The raven-haired, ice-blue-eyed snake was a year *younger* than Triston. Hell would freeze over and implode before he *ever* addressed the vile woman as "Mother."

Huffing, she tapped her slippered toes on the rug covering the floor and pushed her bottom lip out into a pout. "Well?"

Once upon a time, it would have worked on Triston—the innocent-maiden-in-need-of-help charade, but not in over a year. *And never again*, he'd vowed the night he'd caught his father in bed with his betrothed.

He'd like to say it was Esmee's betrayal that had wounded him so deeply he never sought to tie himself to another woman, favoring a life of uncomplicated relationships with no lasting attachments instead.

Mother…it was almost incestuous to think.

She set her hand on his sleeve and gently caressed his arm, sending a shiver of revulsion through him.

"I will accompany my sisters…under one condition." He paused, waiting for her to acquiesce to his demand. When she only smiled as if she'd won some battle he hadn't been aware they were fighting, he continued. "I will bring my own horse." There was absolutely no way he'd willingly share a carriage with Esmee—or anything else for that matter. Though punishing his sisters and diminishing their chances of making suitable matches was not something Triston would carry on his shoulders.

Her smile faltered slightly, but Esmee nodded in agreement. "We shall meet you in the drive." With a flip of her hair, as black as her heart no doubt, she pivoted, calling, "Prudence. Chastity." She punctuated each name with a clap of her hands. "To the carriage with all due haste. Do not be so rude as to keep Triston waiting."

He would wait for eternity if it made Pru and

Chastity happy…what he would *not* do was inconvenience himself to appease Esmee.

This was about his sisters' futures, not pleasing the wolf in sheep's clothing who'd almost duped him into marriage.

He stalked from the townhouse, calling for the butler to have his horse brought round. He would be ready and mounted by the time the women arrived—making further idle chit-chat impossible. To the park, a turn or two down the trail, and he would be on his way.

Blast it all, but he'd managed almost a fortnight without coming into contact with Esmee, and his temper hadn't flared once. Now, with only a moment of conversation his blood boiled again.

A Downshire livery brought round his horse at the same time his sisters' carriage ambled down the alley leading to the stable house.

He swung up into the saddle at the precise moment Pru and Chastity exited the front door, each beaming at seeing him in the drive.

And Triston could not help but return their looks of joy with his own grin.

They wore matching puce-colored gowns with walking boots, cloaks, and each had a fur muff to keep their hands warm. Their curls were pinned back in tight coiffures and garnished with strands of black beads. For not the first time in the last week, Triston wondered how the pair had grown from annoying girls in short dresses with pleats to the women who stood before him. Damn it all, but he wished he still resided at his father's townhouse and could enjoy a bit more time with his sisters before they selected husbands and left home to start their own families—their time for their roguish ancient brother gone.

And he had no doubt, despite their claims to the contrary, that they would marry. They need only find the right men—those who stole their hearts and saw beneath their outward appearances.

Triston was determined to make certain they had enough time in London to do just that.

"We are so pleased you will be accompanying us." Pru accepted the footman's assistance into the open carriage. "We have so missed you the last couple of days."

Triston chuckled. "Drop the demure, proper miss act, Prudence."

Both women looked back at the door, their stepmother still safely out of sight and earshot. Chastity sighed. "We are so grateful you've agreed to come—to save us from an afternoon of lectures on proper decorum during our ride in the park."

"Or another scolding on the proper way to address this lord or that lord."

"Bloody hell, Triston," Pru continued. "The foolish woman thinks to betroth us to men older than Father. Did you hear that? *Older than Father!*"

"And only half as wealthy," Chastity retorted. "She seeks us to be wed and bedded by any old, poor lord who will have us."

"Father will not allow this to happen, I assure you." Triston's words were meant to soothe his sisters' unease; however, even he was uncertain whether their father would be able to put his foot down and stop his newest wife from marrying off Pru and Chastity to unsuitable men. "And if need be, I will step in and rescue you both."

"Rescue them from what, precisely?" Esmee's shrill voice sounded behind them.

His horse paced anxiously as he turned to see the woman, wearing white from her hat all the way to her boots as she made her way down the front steps and to the waiting carriage.

"We were discussing the news that a wild bear has escaped from a traveling sideshow and is said to be roaming Hyde Park."

Both women nodded in unison as if to confirm

Triston's fib.

"Ah, well, it may well be a foot race if that happens." Esmee eyed the pair when the servant handed her up into the conveyance. "And I fear the pair of you would never make it far on foot."

All happiness and excitement drained from both women at their stepmother's cruel comment directed at their ample size.

He cringed as Pru's and Chastity's gazes fell to their laps. "Yes, my lady."

Bloody hell, but he would remove them from the abyss that was their home if he had the power—and the resources.

"Shall we be off?" Lady Downshire signaled for the driver to put the horses in motion as she sat back in her cascade of white. The color represented purity, innocence, and goodness. The woman was none of those things, not now, and not on the fateful day Triston had met her.

Thankfully, he was about to ride ahead of the carriage, cutting off the sight of her and giving him time to diminish his anger. He was here for Pru and Chastity. It was their future that a turn in Hyde Park would improve. He was only here for them, regardless of what anyone thought.

If his presence kept Esmee's spiteful tongue from lashing out at his sisters, then his discomfiture was worth it. It was suspicious he did not notice the woman's many flaws during their brief courtship—he was too overcome by his lust to see that Esmee was not the graceful, adventurous lady he'd thought, but a cunning, manipulative viper.

Triston saw that now—it was all he saw when he looked at the woman.

When they arrived at the most fashionable time to be seen, the park was near to bursting with carriages, horses, vendors, and people walking along the paths. The shouts from orange vendors ripped through the air at the park's gates, and the sound of carriage wheels created a din that echoed through Triston's head.

A bit of his sisters' joy returned as they waved to a friend and then greeted a gentleman who sidled up on his horse. Both girls tittered into their muffs when the lord complimented their upswept hair. However, Esmee cut their conversation short and pushed the carriage onward and away from the lord, who only gave notice to Pru and Chastity.

Triston slowed his horse and fell in line behind the carriage, wanting to keep watch over the girls, but not draw untoward attention to himself. People still openly gawked when he and his stepmother found themselves in the same room—as if the *ton* thought they'd fall back into one another's arms even though his father, the marquis, had solidly won her hand in marriage.

Either that or they thought the Marquis of Downshire would seek to avenge his wife's honor by challenging his son.

Triston would admit to anyone who would listen that his father had done him a grand favor—a boon of epic proportions—by stealing Esmee as he had. If anything, Triston now held a measure of pity for his father to be tied to the she-devil.

The *beau monde* were just as senseless as Lady Downshire if they thought Triston still held a candle of hope for the one he'd once thought himself in love with.

Betrayal had a way of clearing one's muddled eyesight.

And so, Triston tried to remain unnoticed and yet fulfill his obligations to his siblings.

Lady Downshire waved to a cluster of gentlemen standing alongside the carriage path and called to her driver to halt. The gathering of men slowly made their way over to the Downshire carriage, each offering a greeting to Esmee before turning to be introduced to Pru and Chastity. He recognized three of the men, friends of his father, and all as old as his sire.

What was the woman up to? She was supposed to be securing favorable matches for the girls, but she only seemed interested in settling them with older men who were not up to snuff.

The gentlemen said their farewells when Pru and Chastity refused to converse with them, and the carriage started off once more.

Triston kicked his horse into action and rode up alongside the carriage. He was exhausted, he was bored to tears, and this ride in the park had nothing to do with making certain his siblings met men of high caliber. No, this was another performance for Esmee—a way to show all of London how far she'd risen, and that she would never allow Pru or Chastity to wed above her.

"Lord Gaston may only be a baron, but let me be frank, girls, you will likely not do any better," Esmee lectured. "And it would be in your best interest to take your Season seriously. Once I am with child, I will be unable to flit about London with the pair of you, and your father has agreed some time in the country will suit us all until the little lord is born."

The woman's prattling on and on about giving the marquis another child had grown tiresome over the last few months, and Triston could not trust himself to steel a disparaging retort for much longer.

Triston caught Pru's eye and shook his head. "Ladies, I fear the day has gotten away from me, and I have another engagement to attend to. I bid you all good afternoon."

"It was lovely to see you, brother," Pru called with a wave.

"Thank you for accompanying us," Chastity said.

"I will be around again soon." He winked at his sisters, hoping they understood he'd never allow them to be married off to an impoverished baron, nor be relegated to a future confined to their father's country manor. "Enjoy the rest of your ride."

When Pru nodded, Triston knew he was cleared to depart. His siblings understood the restraint it took for him to be around Esmee for any length of time, and they did not take offense to his less than regular attendance.

CHAPTER 6

THE WIND CASCADED across her face, a welcome respite helping to banish the negativity that had come to fill her life of late. She pushed her filly to a trot as the fresh breeze lifted her loose, golden locks. The wind tangled in her tresses, tossing them to and fro, but Edith could care less about the knots she'd have to endure later when her lady's maid put a brush to them.

If it wasn't Luci demanding they more diligently pursue Abercorn to expose his misdeed, then it was Ophelia reminding Edith they only had two days before another article was due. If they did not keep up with their pieces, the *Gazette* would find another gossip columnist to take the place of *Mayfair Confidential*—and that would mean dire consequences for many young, unsuspecting women who thought themselves smitten with a nobleman, only to learn far too late he kept secrets.

Edith slowed her horse's pace, allowing her mother and father to gain some distance as she surveyed them. They rode close, their horses almost rubbing against one another, keeping their hands clasped between them the entire time.

They were in love.

Held a deep, undying commitment to one another.

Shared a life unrestricted by lies, secrets, and betrayal.

They told one another everything, traveled everywhere together, and the only thing they cherished more than Edith was each other—and their mutual adoration.

It was something Luci refused to admit existed, and Ophelia was openly skeptical of.

It was the sole reason Edith would not circulate or back a piece not rooted in solid fact.

Edith could not deny what had been in front of her, her entire life.

Love existed. Commitment was not an elusive trait. And with continued communication and openness, a relationship could flourish and last a lifetime.

Her parents, the Earl and Countess of Shaftesbury, were solid, irrefutable proof.

They gave her hope that one day she, too, would meet a gentleman worthy of her affection and trust. Yet, she hadn't been able to convince Lucianna or Ophelia that every lord was not a cruel, vile man with vices and secrets. If they dedicated a fraction of their time to finding honorable men, then maybe there was hope for all of them.

In the end, Edith was uncertain of Abercorn's role in Tilda's death. Until she was certain, either way, she would continue to help her friends find the answers they sought.

The answers, Edith grudgingly admitted, they all desperately needed.

If she turned her back on their mission, she would not only be turning away from her friends, but she'd also be casting shame on Tilda's memory. They owed it to the girl to find out what had happened to her.

Wherever the facts should lead.

Her head ached at the daunting undertaking she'd agreed to assist Luci and Ophelia with. Her heart hurt for what Luci claimed to have seen; however, her senses demanded they make certain before ruining a man's life. Tilda dying was tragedy enough. There was no need to further compound things by shouting Abercorn's name to all who would listen.

Edith followed her parents as the trail they traveled ended, depositing them back on the main carriage path, still cluttered with fancily garbed men and women in pursuit of social endeavors.

A group of finely dressed men in riding boots galloped across the far grass and around the pond toward Kensington Gardens. And a pair of women hopped out of the way in surprise as the men nodded but continued on. On the trail before her, Edith's parents chatted and laughed, drawing their horses apart to avoid colliding with another horseman. No matter how many times another got in their way, they always drew close once more, their legs almost touching as they rode side by side. They continued on, passing carriage after carriage, but Lord and Lady Shaftesbury never paused to speak with anyone.

Up ahead, a familiar set of brown curls came into view, ensconced in a luxurious open-air carriage with forest green material covering the interior. Edith moved her mare a bit to the right to gain a better view of the conveyance and its occupants.

Why she cared she did not know, but she nudged her horse to quicken her pace as the carriage neared. The broad shoulders and chiseled jawline she'd expected to see across from the two women was not present; instead, Edith was greeted with the back of a midnight-haired woman with a white hat on her head. Over the rear of the carriage, she noted the woman's cloak was also white—a clear contrast to the brown jackets over puce gowns of the women nestled on the seat across from her. The woman in white looked one way, but the other females were focused on something in the opposite direction.

Edith followed their stares, her eyes settling on the

figure she'd hoped—did she truly long to see the man again?—to see in the carriage. He sat tall upon his horse with his chin raised in confidence. He was certainly a horseman with the way he deftly held the reins.

Her stomach fluttered. If she'd been standing, and not astride, her knees would have crumbled beneath her.

Lord Torrington's shoulders were every bit as wide as his horse's hindquarters. It seemed impossible a horse as large as the man existed, yet, Edith could not deny they were a perfectly matched set. The mount was eighteen hands tall if he were one.

If she'd thought Torrington dashing and powerful in evening garb, he was pure strength and dominance astride in riding attire. It was easy to picture the man and his horse charging into battle to fight off opposing soldiers, never pulling back in fear or hesitation.

With a quick wink to the women, Torrington tugged the reins and spurred his mount into a gallop toward the park exit with nary a look for the raven-haired woman.

Edith glanced toward her parents and back at Torrington's retreating frame.

She'd promised her friends a new story—which meant Edith needed to *find* that new story.

Lord Torrington was most certainly the man to give her one. She had no doubt he kept a secret…and she would uncover it.

He was dashingly handsome, obviously wealthy, and born into the grandest circle of society; yet he was unwed. Why was that?

Edith suspected this was where his secret began—and possibly ended.

"Mother!" she shouted above the noise of slow-moving carriage wheels and horse clopping. When her parents turned toward her, Edith continued, "Lady Ophelia and Lucianna have arrived." She pointed to a cluster of horses, carriages, and people all fighting for entrance and departure from the park. "May I continue on with them? They will see me home after."

Edith had never made a habit of lying to her parents—in fact, they rarely gave her an excuse to have to lie.

Her father glanced toward the exit, trying to spot his daughter's friends.

"Please, Father?" she begged. "If I hurry, I can catch them."

She could catch *him*. Lord Torrington was nearly at the gate. If he managed to slip past the crowd and out into London traffic, she'd never find him.

"Edward." Her mother smiled, setting her free hand on her husband's arm. "Allow her to go. It is only a ride in the park, not a night at the opera."

When her father nodded in agreement, Edith called her thanks before sharply pulling her reins and spurring her mare into a fast trot. Glancing over her shoulder, she saw her parents had continued their ride, their attention safely on one another. Edith kicked her mount into a gallop until she reached the exit, desperately trying to keep Torrington's brown hair in sight. It proved rather easy as his mount stood taller than most carriages—and with his added height, the man was in no way inconspicuous. However, Edith needed to be far more subtle in her pursuit if she hoped to follow him unnoticed.

The man would not reveal his secrets if he suspected he was being followed.

As she navigated the crowd, Edith felt for her journal and nub, both securely in the pocket of her gown. Today would be the day she gained some truly worthwhile information to share with Ophelia and Lucianna. It had been nearly a week since she'd discovered the clandestine meeting between the duke, Montrose, and his fair-haired nymph alone in his opera box. It did not appear so scandalous upon first glance until one noticed the woman's bosom was exposed—

and Montrose was set to wed Lady Cavendish in a short three weeks.

She only hoped anything she could find about Torrington was enough to keep her friends occupied and away from Abercorn.

EDITH CONTINUED TO follow Torrington down endless London streets. Her only moment of hesitation was when he crossed the river toward Vauxhall—and ventured into an area known for its crime, poverty, and unsavory entertainments. The notion of turning around and admitting yet another failure was not an option.

As she expected him to keep going—maybe he suspected he was being followed, taking them both on a wild chase—Lord Torrington turned down a narrow lane and slowed his horse to a walk as he maneuvered around a cart loaded with textiles ready for market.

She paused at the end of the lane. There was no conceivable way she could follow him down the narrow path without him noticing her. He must be close to his final destination because it did not appear the lane, truly no more than an alley, led anywhere beyond.

Torrington dismounted his horse about half a block down and flipped the reins to a waiting footman. Why would a servant be waiting outside a building in this part of town?

Once he entered, Edith determined it safe to journey into the alley.

A sign painted on the front of the building Lord Torrington had entered gave the name of the establishment as *Langworth Inn*. The exterior was well kept, the entrance cleared of filth and rubbish. Windows lining the second and third floor were polished clean with their draperies pulled tight. It was in stark contrast to the neighboring buildings, one with not a solid windowpane and another missing its door. The livery who'd taken Torrington's horse had disappeared down an even narrower alley to the side of the inn.

"Ye lost, miss?" A woman pulling a cart of textiles looked up at Edith, her brow furrowed in concern. "I don't be think'n this be the place for ye."

Edith looked back to the inn Torrington had entered—she certainly did not belong here. It only begged the question: what was Lord Torrington, a viscount, doing in this part of London?

He might very well be inside for an afternoon tryst, maybe with a ladybird from Vauxhall. She'd learned recently gentlemen of all ages enjoyed an afternoon with a lovely woman. Imagines of Abercorn and the dark-haired woman sprang to mind, the way her bare rump had been pressed to the windowpane, the devious smile upon her lips, and the laughter she saw brim from the duke. Was that what Torrington was doing at this very moment, enjoying a few brief hours wrapped in a woman's arms? Her heartbeat thrashed in her ears, and her vision clouded for an instant. Edith filled with the urge to kick something.

It was also possible his presence here had nothing to do with a woman and everything to do with business, more accurately, a sham business dealing.

From the appearance of the building, the owner did not lack funds for upkeep, but how could an inn this deep into London remain a profitable endeavor? The lane did not see a heavy flow of traffic, nor was it close to the docks. Could it be the house of an opium den? She'd never seen one, but the *Gazette* had published a story about the insurgence of opiates and those who found pleasure in smoking the nefarious substance. Torrington didn't appear a gentleman who partook in anything stronger than a tumbler of scotch or a pint of ale.

However, there was only one way to find out…she would follow him into the inn.

But first, Edith had to decide if she truly wanted to

know Torrington's secrets.

With a nod, she glanced back at the woman with the cart, still paused before her. "I am not lost, but thank you all the same for your kindness in asking." She gave the woman a reassuring smile. "I am waiting for the servant to take my horse, and then I will be going into the Langworth Inn."

Edith wasn't sure if the words were meant to convince her nothing untoward would happen to her if she dared dismount her horse, or if it was to appease the woman's curiosity.

"Very well, miss," she replied before taking hold of the cart handles. "Ye be careful."

"Thank you." Edith watched the woman pull the heavy cart down the lane before dismounting and peering about. The servant hadn't returned, and she doubted she would be inside long. The street was deserted except for the woman headed to the market.

Edith quickly dismounted her mare and tied the reins to the post outside the inn, knowing full well she could be without a horse when she returned, but she'd promised her friends new information for Ophelia to write about—and she was desperately close to getting it.

There was no turning back now.

The entrance of the inn was as deserted as the street outside. No proprietor waited to greet new customers. No sounds traveled toward Edith from deeper inside the inn. The place certainly was not seeking people looking for accommodations. Highly odd for a place labeled an inn.

A bark of laughter came from the door bordering the stairwell leading to the floors above. Edith inched toward the partially open door, careful to keep her footfalls quiet, and then she peeked into the room. Circular tables were arranged about the space with four stools at each. On the far side was a long bar with an assortment of clear decanters behind it.

A taproom. Edith had never seen an actual

taproom before, let alone entered one.

And today was not the day to explore—she was here for a purpose, and neither of the two men in the room were her objective. One was an older gentleman with his sleeves rolled past his elbows as he poured a pint of ale for a lanky, blond young man who sat on a stool at the long bar.

Neither was Lord Torrington.

She crept a bit closer to make sure she could scan the entire space before stepping back.

A door closed above, and Edith pressed herself against the wall, waiting to be discovered when whomever it was above came down the stairs. She held her breath, fearing she'd be caught and questioned. Turned over to a magistrate and hauled off to a holding house long before she knew what was happening.

Edith hadn't been successful in playing the detective outside Abercorn's townhouse, and she didn't understand why she thought she'd do any better in an inn. On a positive note, there was no chance of her falling from a tree.

When no footsteps sounded on the stairs, Edith sighed in relief.

The cold, rough wall bit into her back even through her many layers of clothing.

She was discovering nothing here, and only risking being caught if either of the men wandered from the taproom.

Hurrying up the stairs, attempting to make as little noise as possible, Edith rushed down the single corridor on the second floor. Room after empty room—a parlor, a library, and a dining room stood open for her scrutiny. The farthest three doors on the floor were solidly closed. She pressed her ear to each, heard nothing, and tried each respective lever. The first two opened easily on well-oiled hinges to reveal empty sleeping quarters. The third was tightly locked.

There was little chance Torrington was on this

floor.

Edith hurried back down the hall and up to the third floor. The hallway looked exactly as the last had: several doors opened to a receiving room, an office, a dining area, and four closed doors at the far end. All entirely uninhabited.

He must be in one of the closed rooms. There was no other place he could be hiding, unless he'd entered the inn and departed out the back. Blast it, but Edith hadn't even thought of that possibility.

No, Edith needed to have faith that Torrington hadn't seen her trailing him, and that he was unaware she was searching for him at this very moment.

She tiptoed down the hall, once again placing her ear to one of the closed doors. Nothing.

She moved on to the next. Silence.

The third, however, proved fruitful. She heard male mumbling from the far side, and something solid hit the floor—a boot, perhaps? The sound was followed by yet another thud.

Images of Torrington undressing surged into her mind, followed quickly by visions of him bare-chested and pulling a carriage with his brute strength. She swallowed, suppressing the need to fan her heated face. She didn't know what she wanted more, to giggle or scold Luci for introducing the foolish fantasy to her mind.

She pressed her ear more firmly to the door, trying her best to decipher his mumbling—or if another occupied the room with him. Damnation, she wasn't even certain it *was* Torrington in the room.

Worse still, Edith couldn't understand what was being said on the far side of the door, although she was fairly certain it was only one voice she heard. Her shoulders sagged with an unexpected release of tension. She'd truly thought to find him here—with a woman.

It was ludicrous she was concerned with what Torrington did or whom he did it with.

He was a stranger—an arrogant, demanding stranger.

Yet, still an Adonis among men.

She shook her head at the thought.

Edith was here to learn what dastardly secrets the man kept, not to spend her afternoon woolgathering over the man's prowess—which she had little doubt was great.

Lucianna would be proud to know that at least Edith wasn't a prude as her mind swirled around images of a certain lord's bare chest.

The squeak of bed ropes sounded as the room's occupant most likely either sat or laid on the bed. And now, Edith was thinking of Torrington's massive frame strewn haphazardly across *her* bed as a pool of heat settled in her most private area. Dash it all, but she was not attracted to the man. And she knew she should not be attracted to him in any way.

She was here to explore his misdeeds, not his body.

"May I help you, miss?" a gentle voice sounded from behind Edith.

CHAPTER 7

TRISTON ALLOWED HIS head to fall into his hands, and he scrubbed away the tension of the day. This was his safe place, where he could just be Triston—not Lord Torrington, not the marquis' son, not the responsible brother of two hoyden sisters, and not a man marred by scandal. No one looked at him with question when he entered this inn. No one inquired as to his hardships. No one demanded anything of him. The place was quiet, and he went undisturbed and unknown to everyone—except his father and his man of business.

It was for this specific reason Triston had chosen the boarding house—and leased the entire third floor—when he could not stand living under his father's roof a moment longer.

Here, he answered to no one.

And, in turn, the inn's other occupants paid him little mind.

As long as no one ventured into his area—except the servants—Triston remained happy with his accommodations. That he did not reside in the most elite area of London only added to the Langworth Inn's appeal. Coming and going, he crossed no one's path unless it was his intention to do so.

A screech sounded outside his door, followed by

the sloshing of water and a tin hitting the wooden floor.

Triston shot to his feet and started for the door.

Water cascaded under his door and reached his bare feet, the lukewarm liquid surely intended for the bath he'd summoned be brought to his room.

He hoped no one was injured.

Pulling the door open, his eyes widened at the spectacle in the hall. Molly, the upstairs maid, scattered to collect the tin she'd dropped, while also attempting to stop the water from traveling farther down the corridor and into other rooms. On her knees, Lady Edith Pelton used her skirts to halt the bathwater from flooding into his room.

The scene would have been highly entertaining if Triston weren't shirtless and barefooted with his trouser flap hanging open in preparation for his bath.

He was indecent, and Edith was so distracted helping Molly, she didn't realize her derriere was positioned perfectly for a pinch as it wagged back and forth as she soaked up the water.

The urge to reach out toward her was strong—as was the need to laugh—but he kept silent and unmoving. Triston relished the opportunity to see how this would play out before him.

"I am dreadfully sorry," Edith gushed. "My friends always speak to my clumsy nature. They will find much enjoyment once again, knowing they have been proven—"

Her voice cut off as Molly stood and stared past her, finally noting Triston's presence.

The time to put the debacle to an end had arrived, accompanied by the stirring in his pants.

"Thank you, Molly," he said with a smile. "I can get this tidied up. You may return to your other chores."

"What—what—what—" she stammered, wringing her hands. "What about your bath, my lord?"

"I am certain it will take some time to heat more water. I can wait." He kept his eyes trained on the servant, hoping she too did not focus on Lady Edith, still on her hands and knees, outside his bedchamber door. "Hurry along."

"Are you certain, my lord?" The maid blinked rapidly, clutching the basin to her chest. What little water remained, dripped down the front of her uniform and pooled at her feet.

He waved her off with a nod. "I am certain, Molly."

With one last glance at Lady Edith, the servant curtseyed and fled back toward the landing.

When Molly had disappeared down the stairs, Triston extended his arm to Edith. "Lady Edith, may I assist you to rise?"

Her shoulders slumped, and her head fell forward, but she did not address him.

"I must say, this is rather more shocking than finding you with your cloak and skirts thrown over your head." He was teasing her unmercifully, and he damn well knew it; however, she deserved any jests he made.

His mind swirled with reasons why Lady Edith was in Langworth Inn, outside his bedchamber door—on her hands and knees. None of them boded well for Triston and his need to remain unscathed by the scandal sheets for the foreseeable future.

His teeth ground together, but he was unable to hold back his rising ire. "What in the bloody hell are you doing here?"

At his harsh words, her shoulders stiffened, and her head snapped up, her eyes moving around to meet his as she pushed to her feet unassisted.

"Do not play coy, my lord," she seethed. "You know exactly why I am here."

It was then she took her narrowed glare from his and moved it to his shirtless chest, her eyes widening. Things would have been safe had her gaze stopped there, but it traveled lower, and her face blossomed with the most fetching rose color as her lips pressed together.

It only made matters worse when his manhood decided to disobey him and harden further as her now wide stare locked on his undone trouser flap.

"I have many ideas why I would *want* you here." He raised his brow in suggestion, though her eyes were still stuck far lower than his face...or chest...or waistband.

She snapped from her daze. "You are incorrigible, my lord," she hissed as she pushed past him—into his bedchamber. Into his empty bedchamber.

He had half a mind to shout for Molly to return and act as chaperone until Lady Edith decided she was ready to depart. Because the way she plopped herself down on his bed, her saturated cloak and skirts clinging to her legs, told Triston she was not leaving anytime soon.

Looking from the blessedly empty hallway to his room and back once more, Triston slammed the door shut. He could not risk anyone happening upon her in his private space.

She'd be compromised.

And he'd be to blame.

"Allow me to ask again, what are you doing here?" No, he was not entirely to blame. Edith had made her own way here, though he hadn't the faintest notion how or why, and she had willingly walked into his chambers and threw herself upon his bed.

All while he stood gawking, trying to remain angry even when his body wanted nothing more than to join her on the bed.

"Why are *you* here?" she retorted, crossing her arms.

"Bloody hell. I live here!"

Edith's muscles went rigid, and she leapt to her feet as if someone had actually pinched her backside. Her head turned from side to side as if noting for the first time that they stood in a bedchamber and she had been sitting upon a bed—a man's bed.

"You live here?" She gulped. "Right outside the

gates of Vauxhall?"

"Langworth Inn is not so close to Vauxhall." His father had had the same reaction when Triston had requested funds to secure his room and board at the Langworth Inn. He was aware the area was not known for much else but entertainment; however, Triston had sought distance and space—between him, society, and his father and the duke's new bride. A little lane off Laud Street had given him exactly what he'd longed for. "And yes, I most certainly do live here. However, you do not."

Even flustered with water dripping from her, she was captivating. Her blond hair was secured in a tight knot at the back of her head with several tendrils framing her face that had escaped her coiffure. He barely stopped himself from stepping toward her and pushing the wayward strands behind her ear.

"You are certainly correct, my lord. And I think it best I depart." She took a step toward the door, keeping her stare on the floor at her feet.

Triston stepped into her path, blocking her exit.

As much as he wanted her gone and away from his private chambers, his need to know why she kept appearing wherever he was proved stronger than his good sense to allow her to pass.

A CHILL RAN down Edith's spine, whether from her water-soaked clothes or the intimidating figure blocking her way, she was uncertain. One thing she knew all too plainly was she'd made a dreadful mistake. She'd thought to spy on Lord Torrington, discover his secrets, and hand them over to Ophelia for exposure by way of the *Gazette*'s *Mayfair Confidential*.

She'd gravely underestimated Torrington, and overestimated her own skill. Spying on him was no easy feat. She was now certain he held some scandalous secret, but she would never be permitted to find out what it was. But, now, Edith doubted she would want to betray the formidable man before her.

There would be consequences—dire consequences.

Edith notched her chin higher, not in confidence but to glare at Torrington straight in the eyes. How dare he deny her departure! "Do step aside, my lord," she hissed, placing her hands on her hips. "I find I wish to leave."

"I think our acquaintance has progressed beyond the 'my lord' formalities." He made no move to allow her escape. "You are in my bedchambers, after all. My given name is Triston."

Triston? Edith wasn't sure why the name surprised her. She'd known his title, but it seemed his given name was an intimacy she was unprepared for, nor had any right to possess.

Hell, at this juncture, she'd half expected his given name to actually be Adonis.

"Oddly, the name suits, my lord." Edith hadn't meant to vocalize her musings, and she quickly looked away to the washstand to his left. If her eyes dropped back to the floor, her perusal would travel all the way down his hulking body—his barely clothed body. And Edith did not need to linger on the way his muscles flexed when he tensed or the speckling of dark hair that covered his chest. Far darker than the hair atop his head. And she most certainly did not want to think about what lay beneath the flap of his undone trousers—for she already suspected it fought to gain freedom. The image caused her face to flush with heat, and her legs to quiver unsteadily.

She shouldn't want to look, but despite her best efforts, her eyes returned to his bare midsection.

Luci would likely whistle at the glorious sight.

Ophelia would swoon into a dead faint, and smelling salts would be needed.

But Edith…Edith hadn't any notion what to do or

what to think. In fact, to her horror, she was frozen. She could not move past him, nor would she retreat farther into his personal chambers. Even now, she was helpless to look away from his muscular shoulders, so wide he could easily carry a fallen carthorse across them. Or maybe rescue an entire schoolhouse of children in one fell swoop.

"Do you enjoy what you see?" he said with a chuckle.

Yet she hadn't actually taken in his form at all, but avoided settling her stare on his finely built masculine body.

She wanted to push him aside and flee, but that would put her hands in contact with his bare skin. Instead, Edith crossed her arms and leaned in close, making it obvious she inspected every inch of him, from his trousers, which hung loosely about his hips, up over his stocky midsection, and finally across his chest and to his face.

"I have seen many oxen with broader shoulders,"—she smirked, pulling back and leaning to the side as if to get a glimpse of his backside—"and far more accentuated hindquarters."

She gulped.

No laughter remained as he narrowed his eyes on her. "Did you just compare my physique to that of a farm animal?"

Edith took a step back—damnation, she would not cower to him. "If you prefer, I can select another animal. A donkey, perhaps? They are well-known for their obstinacy. Or better yet, an African lion, I have read they are intimidating creatures."

"You think me intimidating?" It was Torrington who took a step back this time, as if her words had wounded him. "Wait, do not answer that question—I have a far more important one: why do you keep appearing everywhere I am?"

"It is not I who keeps appearing," Edith corrected.

"I was minding my own business outside of Abercorn's townhouse. You are the one who scared me from the tree. And you were the one who caught my eye in the ballroom. And I was enjoying an afternoon in the park when—" She clamped her mouth shut.

"Enjoying an afternoon in the park until...you saw me and decided to follow?" he demanded. "I may very well be as large as an ox, or as stubborn as a donkey, or even as domineering as a lion, but at least I am not a snake—slithering and sneaking about, ready to bite and poison when the mood strikes."

Edith gasped, covering her mouth with her hand.

"Oh, you find it belittling to be compared to a bloody animal?" he sneered. "Well, I find it insulting to be lied to, followed, and scrutinized by a woman I do not know."

Edith sighed. "I have not been following you, I swear to it."

Not a complete lie, or at least she hadn't been at Lord Abercorn's townhouse to spy on Triston—she allowed herself to think of him by his given name—nor had she attended the ball with Ophelia and Luci expecting to see him. And the park, well, that was rather serendipitous. She had decided to keep an eye on him, but she'd never thought to follow him out of London proper.

Edith glanced to the window, but the drapes were pulled securely shut. "The day must be growing late. My parents will surely be wondering where I am when I don't arrive home on schedule."

"I know what you are up to, Lady Edith Pelton." His stance widened as he surveyed her from head to toe.

It was odd because, Edith was baffled at her bravado in following him and sneaking into the inn; however, she still considered Torrington a friend of Abercorn's, no matter he hadn't admitted as much. He hadn't denied his association with the duke either. She could not allow him to discover her ultimate goal for being outside Abercorn's townhouse, nor her interest in him at the ball. Could she?

No, she needs must distract him from the entire mess she'd created.

It was not only Edith's safety in jeopardy, but also that of Ophelia and Lucianna if the duke found out they persisted in proving his guilt in Tilda's death. He would no doubt seek vengeance if he discovered the truth.

"Why do you not live with your father?" Edith hoped to throw him off guard. "He has a lovely townhouse in a fashionable part of town. It is certainly closer to the more favored parts of London. I imagine it is inconvenient to journey all the way to Surrey for your lodging."

He held his stance, blocking her exit; however, Edith was uncertain she was in any rush to leave. It was highly improper and foolish to remain, but the man and his situation intrigued her.

"I am not the first lord to leave his father's home."

Edith pivoted and sat in a chair close to the fire, hoping her relaxed manner would lull him into an easy conversation. "No, but one does not normally find lodging in such an area." Maybe she could use him to gain information about Abercorn, as well.

His posture loosened, and he paced toward the fireplace and back to the door before swinging around to face her. "I will answer your questions if you agree to do the same."

It was an interesting proposition. "I can ask anything, and you will answer so long as I reciprocate?" she asked, her brow raising. She needed to be certain about what he offered.

It would not do to share information that could be used against her and her friends if she gained nothing in return.

CHAPTER 8

"THAT IS EXACTLY what I am saying, Lady Edith."
Triston was playing with fire, and he damn well knew it.
If he didn't watch out, he was likely to suffer burns that
would not heal with time, only fester and spread.
Though there were no secrets the *ton* and the many
sharp-tongued matrons hadn't used as gossip fodder
since his broken betrothal two years prior. Could it be
the lady before him was oblivious to his past? He
moved from his place blocking the door and leaned
down toward her, placing his hands on each of the
chair's arms before issuing his next warning. "However,
allow me to caution you against lying or misleading me
in any way. I do not take well to such actions."

She stared wide-eyed at his forearms, his position
keeping her seated, before averting her stare to her
worrying hands. Lady Edith tilted her head back and
sighed.

The woman was stalling, and Triston did not have
time for any of it. If she were found alone in his
bedchambers, Edith would be compromised...ruined,
her reputation in tatters. And he would once again be
the spectacle of gossip.

Triston could not allow that to happen; however, if
he did not find out what she was up to, she would

continue to plague him and put herself at risk.

Her eyes drifted shut, and he noticed her hand slip into a pouch in her skirt to grasp something.

"I have one question, Edith," he whispered, still only inches from her. When her eyes sprang open, and her chin tilted back down to meet his gaze, he continued, "Why have you been following me?"

"I told you, I was not—"

"If I am to believe that, then why do you keep appearing near me?"

Edith pulled something from her pocket, it was barely larger than the palm of her hand, but she held it out to him.

"What is this?" Triston took the object, surprised to discover it was a leather-bound book. "You enjoy reading? That tells me nothing."

"Open it," she commanded, crossing her arms defiantly and looking to the small fire in the hearth. "You will find what you need to know within."

Standing straight, Triston moved to the candelabra on his washstand for light and flipped the tiny book in his hands several times. The cover was worn, brown leather with tight stitching along the spine as if it had been repaired recently. One corner bent outward—the place where its owner repeatedly opened it.

Triston did the same, opening the book to reveal a hand-scribed, yellowing page.

Lady Edith's name flowed across the page in large, swirling penmanship.

Was it her handwriting? If so, it was nothing like he'd expected from her. On the several occasions he'd made her acquaintance, or watched her from afar, she always seemed rushed and frenzied. This handwriting was painstakingly neat, as if the writer had much time to dedicate to each letter.

Triston glanced back at her, but the diminishing flames licking the underside of the logs in the hearth kept her attention, giving him a moment to study her—

truly *see* Edith.

Certainly, she was the woman who'd fallen out of his father's tree, the female who'd stared unabashedly across the crowded ballroom at him, and the one who had traversed an unsavory part of London to follow him to Langworth Inn.

But there must be more to this... No woman of gentle breeding would put so much at risk for a lark.

He admired her resolve. As yet, she'd never backed down from him, nor treated him as a fool.

Even now, she seemingly sensed him eyeing her, and her chin notched up.

With her petite frame—at least one-third his size—and her blond hair, she appeared little more than a girl just out of the schoolroom, but on the few occasions he'd garnered a closer look into her almond-shaped, whiskey-colored eyes, he saw a depth no innocent maiden should be burdened with.

But she was here. In his chambers. Sitting calmly.

She hadn't fled as she had during their first meeting, and she'd willingly handed him the book he currently held. Truly, it appeared to be a journal.

Perhaps this was her attempt to seek his help.

Triston turned back to the journal and flipped to the next page. In the same neat script, he read:

Mayfair Confidential

His brow furrowed, and he rolled the words around in his mind, searching, attempting to grasp why the words were familiar to him.

Finally, he shook his head and turned to the next page.

One word was written at the top, a name, underlined several times.

Abercorn.

His sister had told him of Lady Edith's and her friends' connection to Abercorn.

What followed was page after page of barely legible notes. Dates, times, places where Abercorn had been seen. There was even a detailed accounting of people coming and going from his townhouse. Another page, only half-filled, noted both the day he'd discovered her on Downshire property—she'd noted Abercorn had been seen through his top-floor window, consorting with a raven-haired woman—and then continued with notes from the ball when the duke had requested a dance from both Pru and Chastity.

She hadn't lied when she'd argued she hadn't been there because of him.

Why did he feel a pang of resentment that Edith was so wholly focused on Abercorn and not him?

The tightness in his chest released, and his stomach twisted the moment he turned the page to see his name across the top, though it was only underlined once.

Below it was simply written: *built as sturdy as a druid warrior, two sisters (?), does not live with family, friends with Abercorn (?), arrogant.*

Was that the summation of his life thus far?

He should be angry to learn she was also watching him, but Triston was only confused.

"Let me see," he mused. "Built as sturdy as a druid warrior? No, my heritage is closer to a Viking warlord. Two sisters, yes, Prudence and Chastity. Does not live with his family." He paused and glanced around the room. "I think we have established the truth of that. Friends with Abercorn. I believe the term 'friends' is stretching our relationship a bit. We are neighbors. When in London, Abercorn is only the man who lives next door. He has no children or family so, naturally, he dines with us on occasion, but there is nothing more than that between our families. And arrogant? Most certainly. Does that answer all your questions, my lady?" He raised his brow when she turned to stare at him, remaining silent. "Oh, I also had a huge cat growing up…he was a bit of a pest and despised my father, but I loved him all the same."

Triston used his finger and fanned through the rest

of the pages—all blank, awaiting either more information about him or Abercorn. Perhaps she sought yet another man to shadow.

"Can you please put on a shirt?" she asked.

"I apologize if my hulking frame is disturbing your delicate sensibilities," he threw back at her. "I was not expecting company in my private chambers and, therefore, was not dressed appropriately. You must excuse my ungentlemanly attire."

"Do not be ridiculous, my lord," she sighed. "But as enlightening as this has been, I will need my journal back, and then I will be out of your private chambers immediately."

She stood as Triston retrieved a clean linen shirt from his armoire and threw it over his head. "You are not going anywhere yet. I have not gotten my question answered."

Triston sensed he'd reached a delicate topic, one Lady Edith was reluctant to speak about. It was so personal, she seemed prepared to flee without gaining any of the answers she'd come for. However, he had no intention of allowing her to depart yet.

"But—but—," she stammered, her eyes lighting with contempt. "I gave you my journal."

"Which told me what you know about me—and Abercorn—but not *why* you seek this information." Triston tied his trouser flap closed, hoping the gesture would put her at ease. "Now, why *are* you so determined to ruin Abercorn?"

Edith took several quick steps until she stood a mere foot from him and turned her glare up to meet his. "Me, ruin him? He is the one who is responsible for my dear friend's death. I presume the better question here is why *you* would allow your innocent sisters to be in the man's presence for even a moment, knowing the accusations against the man."

"As I said, he is my father's neighbor—a harmless old man with no family to speak of."

"He has been wed three times, and he has outlived them all, even though they are usually decades his junior," Edith seethed, her hands securely on her hips, ready to argue her point. "What say you about that? What if he fancies one of your sisters? What then? Do you plan to accept his offer of marriage and hand your sister over to a man who will likely outlive her, as well?"

"What is your proof Abercorn did anything untoward in his previous marriages?" Triston hadn't many dealings with Abercorn, as the man was nearly old enough to be his grandfather; however, the conviction in Edith's tone swayed him greatly.

"Proof?" she asked. "I was there. I saw my dear, beloved friend lying prone at the bottom of a grand staircase—the *duke's* grand staircase—on her wedding night. A night that should have been the happiest of her life. A day that was supposed to be remembered with great fondness as she and Abercorn set off on their bridal tour. But, instead, Tilda suffered a broken neck from her fall. The physician said she was dead before she hit the bottom step. What other proof do you need? I can sketch the scene for you, if that will make you happy."

Triston had never taken much stock in the accusations leveled against Abercorn. Hell, he'd had enough of his own societal ridicule to last him decades—and within those bits of chatter there had been nothing but a grain of truth, yet that did not stop the gossip mills from feasting on him. He'd heard at White's that the rumors swirling about Abercorn were much the same.

"You saw him push her?" Triston asked, shaking his head. If he heard confirmation, he knew he'd be honor bound to see that Abercorn paid for his crimes.

Edith pivoted away from him and paced toward the door. For a brief moment, he expected her to flee— leaving her journal safely in his hands—but she turned again and paced back toward the hearth. "Of course, I did not see him push her; however, Luci heard them argue at the top of the stairs—she saw him standing above before he fled the hall to return a few moments later when his butler summoned him. Or so Luci has claimed since that night."

Triston breathed a sigh of relief. "No one saw Abercorn physically push his new bride?"

"Well, no, but—"

"And you think spying on the man with your gaggle of friends will find justice for Tilda's death, by ruining a man who may very well be innocent of the crime you have levied upon his person?" He chuckled, harshly. "My own father is married for the third time, and I can attest that he caused no harm to his previous wives, my very own mother included. Abercorn may very well be cursed in love, just as my father is."

"And if one of your sisters perishes because of their association with Abercorn, that blood will be on your hands—the weight on your conscience." Her glare narrowed, but she refused to look away. "I do not know about you, but I will have no other deaths permanently staining my soul if I can make known Abercorn—or any other scoundrel disguised as a gentleman—poses a threat to any woman. My friends and I are determined to save others the fate our friend faced and ended her life."

At some point, either Edith or he had taken a step forward, bringing them from a foot apart, to their bodies almost touching. And so they stood, as several long moments past, neither willing to back down.

CHAPTER 9

EDITH WOULD HAVE been wise to agree with Lord Torrington—Triston—and then tuck her tail and run, not stand toe-to-toe with a man over twice her size, especially with another story due to Ophelia by nightfall.

In that moment, she made the mistake of breathing in deeply, allowing his scent to overtake her. Even with the hint of horse, his scent of amber and dark wood was in no way unappealing to her. Quite the opposite. The raw aroma of Triston had her heartbeat spiking, her chest heaving to gain breath, and she feared her knees would buckle before either of them backed down.

"I will do all in my power to see Abercorn gets what he deserves," Edith hissed, breathing through her open mouth. "I will never allow that man to murder again."

Triston's muddy brown eyes flared with anger, but his tone only held annoyance. "And I cannot allow a man to be ruined without solid proof of wrongdoing."

Thump. Thump. Thump.

"Go away!" Triston shouted. "I am otherwise engaged."

Otherwise engaged. Is that what Torrington called a bitter disagreement with a woman alone in his chambers?

Their standoff was ended as quickly as it had begun when another volley of fistfalls hit the door.

"Open this door immediately, or I will have to call for the maid to bring me a key."

Edith risked a glance at the window. What little light peeked through the slit in the draperies told her the sun was setting and the day was growing late. It would not be long before someone suspected she was not where she should be. Did someone see her leave the park following Triston?

Edith clutched at her chest, her heartbeat increasing. "Who is here?" she whispered.

Triston's jaw clenched tightly as his hand massaged the back of his neck. "My father."

Edith gulped. "Your father?"

"Do not think me too old to kick down this door!" the man called, grasping the latch to the door and attempting to barge in. "Open the bloody door."

The color drained from Triston's normally overconfident face, and his demeanor shifted to uncertainty.

Edith knew the feeling well.

She glanced about the room for a place to hide, yet the bedrails made it impossible to squeeze beneath, and the armoire would not hold more than a small child. As a final resort, she hurried to the window.

"We are three stories above the ground," he hissed from right next to her, startling her. "You may survive a fall from a tree, but if you slipped from this height, you would be no better than your dear departed friend."

"Then where shall I hide?" she demanded in a low tone. "I cannot be found here."

He snorted. "Do you think I do not know that?"

"That is it, Triston!" Footsteps could be heard walking down the hall.

"The dressing closet." Triston set his hands on her shoulders and spun her around to face a door she hadn't realized was there. It was little more than two feet wide—certainly, Torrington could not fit through the opening without turning sideways. "Go. I will handle my father quickly, then you must depart."

Edith didn't waste another moment, but hurried toward the closed door, pulling it open and slipping inside. He closed the door behind her, casting her in complete darkness. Yes, she knew the tiny room was likely littered with boots, ballroom shoes, shirts, cravats, and trousers; however, the notion of not knowing for certain was daunting. Pressing her ear to the wood, Edith heard Triston move toward the door and as he unlatched it, and used the sound to cover her own opening of the dressing room door a crack.

From her vantage point, she could not see anything but Triston's hand pulling the portal wide, and a glimpse of a large man—nearly as tall as Triston—stepping into the room.

The door shut behind him, cutting off the light from the hall beyond.

Footsteps sounded, and Edith feared that Triston's father suspected someone hid within the room, and was set on finding her. She took a step back, deeper in the closet and away from the voices. Though, even if she ducked behind the pressed and hung shirts would she not be hidden entirely from view.

"Father, to what do I owe this visit? I was under the impression our meeting this morning was sufficient to count toward your forced weekly conversation." Triston's words dripped with sarcasm. "Am I wrong?"

"You did not show up to escort Prudence and Chastity to their evening entertainment," his father responded with a hint of jest. "I asked three things of you: fall in line, accompany your sisters, and do not outshine their endeavors to find suitable husbands. Why in the bloody hell is that too much to ask?"

Edith stepped forward once more, needing to see Triston's reaction to his father's harsh tone. The need to exit the closet and stand at Triston's side was almost overwhelming. That would not help either of them and would only go to proving his father correct.

"I escorted the girls—and Lady Downshire—to Hyde Park after I left our meeting," Triston countered. "I only just arrived home an hour ago, and I am awaiting a bath. I planned to come for them immediately after."

Edith knew they'd been speaking for more than an hour. It was her fault Triston had failed to appear for his sisters.

"I will dress immediately and come for them; the evening is still early."

Edith saw the elder man wave his hand in dismissal. "Do not bother, Esmee dressed and escorted the pair."

"Father, I—"

"Do you think I allow you to live here and still collect an allowance because of my kind nature?"

Edith shrank back from the opening when footsteps sounded on the wooden floor, coming in her direction.

"Would you prefer I live under your roof and have to see the woman who betrayed me"—the door slammed shut, muffling his response, yet she could still decipher some words—"...did you...my betrothed...seducing her."

"I fear you should not gain too much familiarity with your accommodations, Triston." The other man shouted loud enough to penetrate the thick wooden door separating Edith from the confrontation in the next room. "If you are unable to fulfill my demands, you will be living under my roof once more. Unless you have some source of income I am unaware of."

Triston said something in response, and from the lowering of Lord Downshire's voice, Triston must have conceded to his father's edict.

Edith moved deeper into the dressing closet to think over all she'd heard thus far. What had Triston meant by his utterance regarding the betrayal by his betrothed and someone else seducing her? Maybe he *did* have secrets, and Edith just hadn't known where to look or what questions to ask. The story certainly revolved around why Triston resided in a boarding house and not his family home.

Edith hastily spilled her hand into the sewn-in pocket on her skirt, but it was empty but for the nub she used to write. Blast it all, but Edith wished she hadn't given the journal to Triston, or left it in his possession when he'd rushed her into the dressing room. These were all things she need remember and ask about later.

The door swung open and crashed into the frame, casting muted light on the small space. Edith let out an unladylike screech as she nearly leapt out of her skin, her foot knocking a stack of boxes over, spilling their contents on the closet floor. As quickly as the light flooded into the room, it was blocked once more when Triston stood in her path, his large body framed by the doorway.

With the fire from the hearth lighting his back, he appeared truly fearsome, yet Edith refused to shrink in terror.

He'd had plenty of opportunities to harm her, and he hadn't.

She snatched her journal from his hand and pushed past him. "What was all this about?"

Edith didn't turn to see his reaction but moved to the window and pulled the drape aside to view the front of the inn as Lord Downshire entered his carriage and sped off. Edith made certain to keep behind the heavy window covering to shield herself from sight. Surprisingly, her horse was still tethered to the post where she'd left the mare. Not surprisingly, the sun had set, and the street was dark, except for the light coming from the windows of the inn.

The afternoon had passed, and her parents must be

worried about her. Not to mention Lady Lucianna and Ophelia.

"It is time you leave, Lady Edith." The words were whispered near her ear, and a tingle traveled down her back.

She'd asked Triston a question, but with the feel of his breath upon her neck and his heated body so close to her back, she couldn't remember what it was she wanted to know.

HE SHOULDN'T BE standing so close to her.

He shouldn't have allowed her into his bedchambers.

He shouldn't have attempted to trick his father into an argument.

He shouldn't be surprised that he longed to wrap his arms around the petite, determined, headstrong woman before him. If he were completely out of his mind, he would turn her toward him, take her into his arms, and lay her gently across his bed, showering her entire body with kisses, evidence of the need he hadn't realized he felt for her until now.

A thirst he hadn't felt for any woman since Esmee's betrayal.

Triston needed her gone, immediately. He couldn't worry about her future plans for ruining Abercorn, nor what she'd overheard about Triston's past.

He grasped her hand where it pulled back the drapery, revealing the street beyond and his father's departing carriage. Unfortunately, the movement brought her even closer. Her hair smelled of jasmine and honeysuckle. He knew the fragrances well, they were the same scents his mother favored and were what he'd gifted to his dear sisters the prior Christmastide morning.

His mother was a fine woman. His sisters, even

though they didn't share the same mother, were also noble and kind.

Trustworthy.

Jasmine and honeysuckle reminded Triston of trust.

Esmee's preferred aroma had been dark—berries and bergamot.

The last person he wanted to be thinking of while Edith was so close was Lady Downshire.

Triston leaned closer to Edith's neck and breathed deeply once more, allowing the scent to overtake him. He'd never thought the fragrance a woman chose could speak to their nature.

"I should go." Edith pulled her hand from the drape—and his touch—and turned.

In that moment, they were body-to-body, her bosom pressed securely to his abdomen and her head tilted back so far it could not possibly be comfortable.

"That would be wise, Lady Edith."

"Before anyone sees me here."

"There is most certainly risk of that," he breathed as his arm circled her waist.

"And then we would be in far more danger than we are at present."

Odd, but Triston could not imagine a more dangerous position than this very moment with Edith pulled tightly to his chest. All he need do is lean down and take her lips, but that would cause him to step back, putting distance between their bodies.

Triston wanted nothing between them.

She stared up at him, her eyes begging him to hold her close even as he noticed her body pulling away from him.

"Bloody hell, Edith." He stepped away, intending to let her go, bid her to leave with all due haste, but his body did not listen. His head dipped, and his lips met her soft, plump mouth at the same time his arms wrapped around her once more and lifted her to meet his great height. She weighed no more than a feather in his embrace. "Edith," he moaned against her lips, scared to pull back and have her float away from him.

Her fingers threaded through his hair, tightening and tugging as he deepened their kiss, he dared to drag his tongue along her bottom lip. Her entire body tensed before she quivered in his arms.

Triston released her and pulled back, staring down at her.

Her fingers, no longer entangled in his hair, now pressed to her reddened lips.

"I think it best I depart," she mumbled, her free hand finding her hidden pocket and the journal most likely within once more. "I am sorry for keeping you from your sisters, my lord."

"Allow me to change, and I will accompany you home." His heart nearly beat from his chest. It would be a cold day in hell before he allowed her out of his sight, especially to travel about darkened London streets. He was a gentleman, after all. And *if* it had to do with anything deeper, Triston wasn't willing to think of that now. "It will only take me a moment."

"We both know that is unwise."

She stepped away from him, toward the door, and an entirely new void opened within him.

"I cannot, in good conscience, allow you to leave unchaperoned."

"And I cannot, in good conscience, allow anyone to know I was here."

Was that sorrow in her eyes? Did she want to stay with him as much as he wanted her to remain?

With one final look, she hurried to the door and slipped out.

The sound of her riding boots could be heard running down the hall and taking to the stairs.

Triston sprang into action and was out his door and turning the opposite way Edith had fled. Bloody hell, but she was right. She could not risk being seen alone with him—he understood that much; however, that did not mean he'd allow her to flee into the night without someone to watch over her.

Pushing the door at the end of the hall wide, he shouted, "Ames!"

"Are ye ready for ye bath, m'lord," his manservant asked from the depths of the servants' stairwell. "I can be right up with a basin o' water."

"Ames, have Molly bring the water," he commanded into the darkness below. "I want you to follow the woman who is departing out front. Make certain she arrives home safely."

"I will, m'lord." Ames's feet could be heard shuffling into his boots before a door slammed, and Triston knew his manservant would not disappoint him.

Triston's father had insisted if he wanted to keep his residence at Langworth Inn, he needed to heed Downshire's every wish. And tonight, he'd failed, leaving his sisters to be escorted to the ball by Esmee.

He was torn between following Edith home and washing quickly to attend to his sisters, to get back into his father's good graces. The marquis had told Triston not to bother with the girls this evening, that Esmee was with them. But Triston knew better than to believe his father. The older man still expected his son to hurry and attend to his duty.

Triston had an obligation to Prudence and Chastity—which, most certainly had nothing to do with his father's demands—but after, he would call on Lady Edith and command her to let go of her foolish notion to uncover Abercorn's misdeeds. If the man were truly dangerous, the last thing Triston wanted was Edith—and her friends—anywhere near him.

CHAPTER 10

EDITH STARTLED AWAKE to complete darkness—and stale air.

Her entire body stiffened with alert even as fear as hot as a flame coursed through her.

Something caressed her cheek and lips. She wanted to push into the feeling, remember the way Triston's mouth had felt against hers and slip back into the dream she'd been in before waking.

Had she fallen asleep in his dressing closet? No, she'd departed Langworth Inn. Edith was certain of it. Right after Lord Downshire had left, in fact. She'd sprinted to the stairs and out the front door without anyone noticing.

Her head ached when she tried to concentrate on what had happened next. Something pushed incessantly into her hip, causing an agonizing discomfort. Her mind continued to roll, a stark terror settling around her like a well-tailored cloak as she tried to identify her location.

Shifting, Edith realized she couldn't move hands. They were held securely in front of her, her palms facing one another with her fingers clasped. Another excruciating jab sent shooting pain into her side and up into her back at the same time her head throbbed. It was the rough wood below her digging into her side, her hands tied at her waist making it impossible to push off her hip to her back.

A numbness overtook her as her denial settled in.

Edith opened her mouth to scream, but nothing moved past the lump lodged in her throat. Utter disbelief swiftly transformed into panic as her voice ripped from her chest. The high-pitched scream echoed in her confined space, causing terror to take hold.

A bout of dizziness brought spots of bright colors—red, green, and yellow—before her eyes, and her stomach roiled.

She couldn't think clearly, unable to grasp where she was and how she'd gotten here.

Her entire body shook and her teeth chattered—though if it was from the cold or her fright, Edith wasn't sure.

She bent her elbows, bringing her hands to her head. Her fingers clawed at whatever covered her face—a coarse fabric that smelled of hay, causing the stale air that infused her lungs and kept her short of breath. Pushing upward on the hood, she was able to move it high enough to gain a proper breath, yet it did nothing to dispel the staleness of the air surrounding her.

Her heart raced erratically, and her entire body trembled intensely.

Edith opened her mouth to scream once more…or call for help, but the words stuck in her suddenly dry throat.

She attempted to straighten her cramped legs, which protested the sudden movement, causing her head to pound ever more. Thankfully, her ankles were not bound.

The floor beneath her jolted and bumped, raising her body from its place only to send it crashing down again, sending her squarely onto her bruised hip and knocking her shoulder.

It returned quickly to the even sway from before.

Though the gentle motion did nothing to dim the

increasing pain taking over her body from her head to her shoulder and down to her hip. She prayed for the numbness of moments before to return and take it all away.

Yet, she remained awake and alert to every shooting ache coursing through her.

Pushing the hood higher still, she noted the space wasn't as dark as she'd thought. She spied a crack above her head and shifted to her back to gain a better look. Light could be seen above—its brightness coming and going as if swinging like a pendulum.

Back and forth. Back and forth.

Edith focused on the pattern, her screaming mind quieting for a brief time. She released her clasped fingers, tracing the sway of the light in the few inches of movement her ties afforded.

She hastily turned to her side once more when her head exploded in pain and her stomach threatened to revolt.

Reaching out with her bound hands, she felt the darkened space before her—wood, the same as beneath her and at her feet.

It was like she was stowed in a box. A cold, icy chill ran through her.

But there was light from above and a constant jostling as the wooden enclosure moved.

Bringing her legs high, Edith kicked out at the wood above her, but was only rewarded with a shower of dirt falling upon her. Her eyes burned from the filth as she blinked it away, bringing her hands up to scrub at her face. Whatever kept her locked in this tight space was as securely fastened as her hands were bound.

Would anyone realize she'd disappeared? Would someone look for her? If she had no idea what had transpired or where she was headed, how could she expect anyone else to figure it out?

Edith needed to concentrate. Closing her eyes once more, she begged her mind to stop swirling, her panic to subside, and listened to the sounds around her. She needed to think—what was she hearing? What was she feeling?

The churn and fall of carriage wheels along a dirt road. She was in a carriage...the boot of a traveling coach.

The creak of the lamp as it swung on the rear of the carriage...above her head.

Someone had taken her, but why?

Suddenly, Edith remembered detouring away from her home in Mayfair—toward St. James.

Her terror returned with a vengeance, and she shrank into herself, pulling her knees as close to her chest as her skirts allowed.

She vaguely remembered guiding her horse down Abercorn's street, hoping to learn something, anything, for when she returned home, she was certain her parents' fright over her disappearance would quickly morph to anger. Her freedom to travel about London without their attendance would be no more. And so, instead of returning home immediately after leaving Triston, she'd thought to make one last attempt with Abercorn. The possibility of dismounting her horse and knocking on his door had even crossed her mind as a rational course of action.

Unfortunately, Edith didn't recall making it to Abercorn's door.

She squeezed her eyes tighter. She needs must remember what had happened...or anything that would tell her where she was and who'd taken her.

The evening had been darkening, the sun already having fallen behind the tall buildings of London proper. Edith had passed a carriage on her way down St. James, but the curtains were pulled tightly, and she couldn't see within, although the coachman had nodded to her as they passed.

The Abercorn townhouse had come into view—the house ablaze with light as if His Grace were home for the night or had yet to leave. Edith had dismounted her mare and tied it to the tree she now knew resided on Downshire property.

A sound came from behind her, a stick breaking, and then...blackness.

That was all.

Instead of attempting to evoke anything else, Edith focused once more on where she was at present. Her head throbbed again as if trying to block any further memories from resurfacing. The pounding only managed to increase her fear, the hair on her neck standing on end, and her muscles screaming for movement. Panic raced through her, begging Edith to do something—fight to gain freedom, kick, and scream. Whatever it took to break from her prison.

She tried once more, kicking her feet up with as much force as she could muster from her position. But the boards didn't give and the movement only sent waves of throbbing pain up her legs to her shoulder and hip.

Immense pain clouded her vision.

She was in a carriage, that much she was now certain of. With only the sounds of the wheels turning, the horses' hooves, and the swinging of the lamp above the boot, Edith suspected she was not in London proper any longer. There were no voices to be heard, no shouts from passing carriages, or calls of warning from pedestrians walking along the street. The carriage jostled along the uneven road as it hit ruts and bumps along the way. The reins jingled against one another as the conveyance turned sharply.

Edith scooted toward the side and pressed her eye close to another crack in the wood. The glow from the lamp afforded her a view behind the carriage—nothing but the empty road with trees bordering each side and shrubs growing large enough to block the path behind them.

Thankfully, with her nose also pressed to the side

of the boot, her lungs breathed in fresh, clean air, relieving the pressure in her chest. With the fresh breath came something new—a scent she hadn't smelled in many years. Crisp, cold salt.

Whoever had taken her was bound for the sea.

CHAPTER 11

TRISTON STRAIGHTENED HIS cravat as he surveyed the ballroom, attempting to locate his sisters. It would have been wise to remain at Langworth Inn long enough for Ames to return and assist him with his evening attire—and confirm that Lady Edith had arrived home safely. Many would argue Triston was not always a wise man—of that he needed no convincing. Along with his hastily tied neckcloth, Triston's brown jacket did not precisely match his darker trousers—a fact he had not been aware of until he entered the ballroom and the hundreds of candles above illuminated his improper wardrobe selection.

Blast it all but he'd been unable to take his mind from Lady Edith—and their kiss—followed by her quick departure. Not a piece of him had wanted to see her go. Not long before their kiss, he'd been infuriated with her; however, a simple embrace—that was in no way simple—had extinguished his anger and flared another emotion entirely within him.

She'd compared him to an ox—and a druid warrior—an arrogant ox with dubious friends.

Everything had transpired so rapidly, Triston hadn't made the connection between the first page of her journal and the *London Daily Gazette* until he'd called for his carriage to be brought round.

Mayfair Confidential.

It was a weekly column in the *Gazette*, nothing more than unfounded gossip, though the writer claimed to have substantiated all stories. To Triston's satisfaction, the column hadn't come to be until *after* his own brush with scandal.

He'd been shocked and insulted to think Edith had set her sights on him, gone to the great risk of embroiling them both in a new scandal, all for a story. She'd be disappointed to learn, as gentlemen of the *ton* went, he was a rather boring fellow. Triston had seen enough upset and heartache to last him a lifetime. Certainly, he enjoyed himself on occasion, but nothing scandalous or noteworthy; especially with Pru and Chastity joining the marriage market this Season.

Speaking of Prudence and Chastity…he spotted his sisters on the far side of the ballroom, once again hidden behind a large palm.

He shook his head at their foolish notion of remaining unseen until they were ready.

Did they not understand what was at stake if they did not settle on matches this Season? There would not be a next for them. It had taken all of Triston's persuasive tactics to convince his father to allow the girls at least one Season before Esmee became with child and she insisted they all move to the country until after the babe was born. There was no guarantee his father's wife would allow his siblings a future Season after.

Regardless, he was surprised to see Pru and Chastity alone.

He scanned the crowd once more, looking for a familiar raven-haired witch, but a far different—but no less deadly—stare met his. Her eyes not icy blue but a deep emerald.

Before he had enough sense to flee, Lady Lucianna and Lady Ophelia strode in his direction.

If he were a wise man, which he'd even more come to believe he was not, Triston would turn now, return to his lodgings, and not venture into society again.

"My lord," Lady Lucianna hissed, stopping before him, unconcerned a proper introduction had yet to be made between them.

"Lady Lucianna, I have heard a great deal—"

Her narrowed stare had his words catching in his throat.

"Where is Edith?" Lady Ophelia asked, her wavy, deep red hair far more fiery than her words.

"Why in heavens name would you presume I know anything about Lady Edith's whereabouts?" he posed.

He knew his mistake immediately when Lady Lucianna snorted and crossed her arms, and Lady Ophelia gasped, pressing her fan to her chest before quickly snapping it open to cool her face.

"We know she has been keeping an eye on you," Lady Lucianna continued. "We were to meet before the ball, but Lord and Lady Shaftesbury said she left Hyde Park earlier under the guise of spotting us."

"But we were not at the park today," Lady Ophelia replied, looking to Lady Lucianna for reassurance. "And Edith never returned home. Her parents came around looking for her."

Lady Lucianna kept her glare on him. "Which means, she followed *you*."

"This is preposterous," Triston retorted. He didn't want to mention the likelihood that Edith following Abercorn was just as convincing as the theory Lady Lucianna had settled upon. An inkling of unease settled in the pit of his stomach, despite his proclamation. He slammed his hands into his pockets and rolled back on his heels. "There is no way you can know I was at Hyde Park today."

"Oh," Lady Lucianna cooed, and Triston suspected she was about to snap the trap shut around him. "Lady Prudence and Lady Chastity were more than happy to share the news of their ride in the park today…accompanied by you, my lord."

Triston glanced between the two women, each with their brows raised in question as if they'd expected him to lie and were happy to confront him with the damning proof he'd requested. There was little use denying it. While they suspected Edith had followed him from the park, he knew she had.

But she'd departed Langworth Inn almost two hours prior. That was plenty of time for her to dress and attend to her friends, yet, Ames hadn't returned before Triston had departed. He did not know for certain she'd arrived home without anything going awry.

"Where is she, Torrington?" Lady Lucianna took a menacing step toward him. While the woman was very thin, her height rivaled his. "I can see you know something you are not telling us."

It was none of their concern if Triston were hiding something from them; however, it had been his responsibility to make sure Edith arrived home safely— and he'd forsaken her. He'd failed, as he had with so many things in his life. The notion of pleasing everyone, doing exactly what an honorable gentleman would, was daunting. And everything had gone wrong again. Perhaps he would be wise to not put so much time into helping others. It never seemed to work out.

"I do not think he is going to tell us what we need to know," Lady Lucianna mused. "Ophelia, I think it is time we send for the magistrate. Allow him to handle things before Torrington has the opportunity to change his story and consort with his sisters to gain their cooperation in the matter."

"If you do that, I will tell all of London that Lady Edith is behind the *Mayfair Confidential* column in the *Gazette*." Triston watched the pair closely. He suspected Edith was not the only one behind the column, and he highly doubted her friends would allow her to take the fall if society placed the blame solely on her.

Neither woman moved.

Lucianna scowled at him, her brow wrinkling in displeasure, while Lady Ophelia once again looked as if she'd faint if she did not gain a spot of fresh air.

"Now—" It was Triston's turn to glare. "I think it best we step outside and discuss this matter...in private."

The young women looked to one another before nodding in agreement.

"Since I arrived only a few moments ago, my carriage should still be waiting out front. I will meet you both there after I inform my sisters I will not be able to remain."

"You will come promptly?" Lucianna asked. "This is not yet another charade?"

"I promise to not tarry overlong."

"Ophelia, tell your mother you are ill and I will escort you home," Lady Lucianna instructed. "And I will give my father a similar excuse."

"That is wonderfully ingenious, Luci," Ophela squealed before heading off in the direction of the refreshment table.

"We will wait at your carriage." With a final glare, Lady Lucianna turned in search of her own family.

Triston scanned the crowd once more. His sisters hadn't noticed his arrival yet, and blast it all, he couldn't locate Esmee in the crush.

Edith could be in danger; he had no time to waste in finding her.

His gut screamed Edith had been speaking the truth all along—that Abercorn was indeed a threat. Though, just hours before, he would have assumed it just as likely she'd be set upon by thieves on the London streets as it would be that Abercorn meant anyone any harm. He'd been a fool to dismiss her concerns so swiftly.

Finally, Prudence and Chastity caught his stare and hustled over to him.

"You have arrived," Pru sighed.

"Guess who spoke to us. You will not believe it," Chastity gushed.

"I do not have time to chat, dear sisters," Triston said, continuing to search the room. "Where is Lady Downshire?"

"She deposited us here and demanded we act accordingly until your arrival." Prudence narrowed her gaze on him, likely noting his tense shoulders. "She said you would see us home safely at the end of the night. Why do you ask?"

Blast it all. Triston did not have time for any of this. It was quite possible that Edith had arrived home without incident, but he needed to know for certain. However, he could not leave his sisters here without a chaperone, or a means to arrive home.

"You needs must come with me." Triston pivoted and started for the door, not waiting for any response. "Come along."

His sisters burst into action and followed quickly behind him as he exited the ballroom and departed the front door.

"Our wraps!" Chastity cried, but didn't pause to wait for the servant to find and return them.

"Come," Prudence hissed. "Something is afoot and I, for one, want to find out what. Triston is never in such a tizzy."

A tizzy? At any other time, he would have chuckled at Pru's use of the word, but not this day. He *was* in a tizzy…soon to be a frenzy if they didn't locate Edith with all due haste.

Just as he'd requested, Lady Lucianna and Lady Ophelia waited by his carriage.

Bloody hell, but Triston hadn't realized he'd be sharing the carriage ride with not only Edith's close friends but also his sisters. Four women in one carriage.

They all seemed surprised to see one another.

Pru's and Chastity's surprise showed in overexcited

shouts of glee, while Lucianna and Ophelia gave him quizzical looks but greeted his sisters kindly.

"What is amiss?" Pru asked, taking Lucianna's hands in hers. "Triston is fairly out of his mind with worry."

"As he should be." Lucianna threw an accusatory frown in his direction. "But what are the pair of you doing here? You should be enjoying your evening at the ball."

"I am depositing them at home before we set off for Lady Edith's townhouse." Triston signaled for his coachman to set the steps down for the woman to enter. "Can we be off?"

"Lady Edith Pelton?" Chastity whispered to Ophelia. When the auburn-haired woman nodded in confirmation, his sister clapped her hands in anticipation. "Must we go home, brother?"

"Yes!" Triston replied in unison with both Lady Lucianna and Lady Ophelia. He cleared his throat and lowered his tone. "We will drop you at home, and I promise to gladly escort you wherever you demand in the future."

Pru and Chastity gave him mirrored pouts as he swung his arm wide, motioning for them to enter the carriage.

"Take us to the Downshire townhouse, quickly, if you please," Triston commanded.

Triston took his seat between his sisters with Edith's friends sitting opposite. They tried not to scowl at him and keep their questions unvoiced until they deposited Pru and Chastity, but they were failing miserably at both.

All while Triston attempted to keep his unease at bay.

"Tell me what you know," he demanded. His sister's presences be damned.

"Why do you not tell us what *you* know first?" Lucianna notched her chin high.

"This is outlandish." Did they not understand he cared about Edith as much as they did? He'd known full well the risks she was taking spying on Abercorn, and yet he'd thought the situation harmless, all things considered. As far as Triston was concerned, Abercorn wasn't a scoundrel. He wasn't a man prone to violence. Triston would have known, would have heard something. "Lady Edith did, in fact, follow me from the park this afternoon—all the way to my lodging."

Chastity gasped beside him. "All the way across the river?"

Lucianna and Ophelia shared a skeptical glance. "And what did you do when you found her at your lodging?"

"Yes, brother," Pru begged, clasping her hands. "What did you do?"

Triston was uncertain what luck he still possessed, but mercifully, they arrived at his father's townhouse then. The coachman pulled into the drive, but Triston didn't wait for him to climb down from his perch; instead, he opened the door himself and leapt to the ground.

Holding his hand out, his sisters stepped down one at a time.

"Is Lady Edith in danger?" Pru wrung her hands before her, knotting the handle of her handbag. "Tell me you have naught to do with this. We only just met Lady Lucianna and Lady Ophelia."

"We desperately want to call them friends." Chastity set her hand on his sleeve.

"I cannot say if Edith is in danger or not, but I can assure you, I have nothing to do with her disappearance." He placed a quick kiss to each of his sister's cheeks. "Now, allow me to see you to the door."

His father stood in the doorway when they arrived. "What is the meaning of this?"

"I must return the girls a bit early due to an unforeseen incident." Triston squared his shoulders, prepared for his father's wrath. The man did not disappoint.

"What have you done now, Triston?"

"I cannot speak to the matter at this moment, Father, but I will tell you as soon as I know exactly what has transpired."

"Yes, Father," Pru said, coming to his defense. "It is a grave matter indeed."

"Where is Esmee?" Downshire peered over Triston's shoulder. "Why did you not leave the girls in her care?"

"Stepmother did not remain with us at the ball," Chastity said.

"She instructed us to keep out of trouble until Triston arrived to see us home."

His father eyed Pru and Chastity, a hint of question in his glare. However, though the man always thought the worst of Triston, he loved his children and never questioned his daughters when they spoke.

"Callahan!" Downshire shouted. "Where is Lady Downshire?"

His father's aging butler appeared in the foyer, his lips pressed together in a grimace as his eyes ping-ponged from Triston to Downshire to the girls.

"I must take my leave, Father." Triston gave the man a curt bow. He had no intentions of remaining to hear about Esmee's latest flight of fancy. "Again, I am sorry you had to leave the ball this evening."

"Do not fret," Chasity replied, stepping forward to squeeze his hand. "We only hope you find her."

"Find who?" Downshire demanded as Triston turned to depart.

"We will tell you all, Father."

"My lord?"

Triston halted at the unease in the butler's voice.

"My lady returned after dropping Lady Prudence and Lady Chastity at the ball. I saw her lady's maid rush a large satchel to the marchioness's waiting carriage."

It was nothing more than his father deserved. Esmee was leaving him and running away with another. Much as she'd done to *him* two years prior. He'd begged his father not to trust the viperous woman, but he'd needed to discover the fact on his own.

"Did she tell you where she was headed?"

"I believe her maid said she'd be away for several days."

Triston shook his head. He could not concern himself with his father's hellion of a wife—he had his own wayward woman to find.

Without another wasted moment, he stomped from the house. Movement next to his father's townhouse caught his eye. A horse was tethered to the tree Edith had fallen from over a week prior.

Triston hurried to the animal—a mare.

She pranced in place anxiously.

What was the horse doing here? Edith must be close, possibly eavesdropping on Lord Abercorn once more, but no light shone from his townhouse's windowpanes. There was no way she'd leave without her horse…especially after the sun had set. She must be close.

His heart spiked as he scanned the area. Maybe she'd decided to climb another tree and she'd fallen again—this time injuring herself.

On the ground, not far from the tethered beast, Triston spotted something familiar.

Edith's journal!

She would never depart without her notes.

Triston pushed a leaf from the leather-bound book and picked it up.

"What is it?" Lady Lucianna had departed the carriage and stood a few paces from him. "It looks to be Edith's mare, Poppy."

Triston could not nod, not without taking his stare off the journal he held.

He attempted to flip open the book, but his finger

slipped on something moist marring the cover.

It was too dark to see properly, but he brought his wet finger to his nose.

Salt...and copper. He rubbed his forefinger and thumb together. The liquid making his skin sticky.

Every sense Triston possessed heightened. The night breeze rustled a patch of fallen leaves, the horses neighed to be returned to their warm stables, and his entire body hummed with anticipation.

Panic? Dread? Rage?

Triston allowed each to overtake him in due course. He lived a thousand days in a blink of an eye.

"Is that..." Ophelia gasped, obviously following Lucianna from the carriage.

"Blood?" Lucianna finished.

CHAPTER 12

EDITH'S FINGERS ACHED from trying to pry a nail loose from its hole. The continued bumps and dips in the road did nothing to lessen her pounding headache or the burden on her shoulder and hip. The area was in no way large enough to gain a sitting position.

She groaned, shifting once more to better shield her shoulder.

It was still dark outside, the morning sun not yet risen, but other than this, Edith had no notion if it were midnight or approaching sunrise.

In the hours she'd spent attempting to find a way out of the boot—and the moving carriage—she'd discovered the source of the punishing pain in her head. A knot had formed at her hairline—she'd been hit with something, splitting her skin.

Her ice-cold fear had thawed to frustration.

She'd screamed until her throat was raw. She'd begged to be released with no answers. She'd kicked, pounded, scraped, and banged at the wood surrounding her until every inch of her body ached with unseen bruises.

As the seemingly endless moments passed, Edith determined there was no possibility she'd break herself loose. The best she could do was conserve her strength and hope to gain her freedom once the carriage arrived at its destination.

How had she gotten herself into such a predicament?

The worst part was that Torrington had warned her against spying on Abercorn, had implored her to give up her daring determination to ruin the duke. But Edith hadn't listened. She'd been so focused on making right what had happened to Tilda and helping to prove Luci's accusation correct, she hadn't thought through the risks of her endeavor. Or what might happen if she were caught.

Which, from her current predicament, she had been.

However, did that mean Abercorn *was* guilty of pushing Tilda down the stairs on their wedding night?

If he'd taken her, then it was all the proof society needed to condemn him for his treacherous actions. If she'd live to prove his culpability was an entirely different matter—one Edith was determined not to dwell on.

She only need survive this—but how long would it be before someone noted her disappearance?

If Luci and Ophelia went to her parents after Edith failed to show for their meeting, would anyone have faith in the pair that something untoward had occurred? They'd cried foul once before, and no one had believed them. Would their words of concern be cast aside as quickly as their accusations against Abercorn?

Edith should have stood by Luci's side on the night Tilda died. Shouted as loudly as she could about Abercorn and his involvement—she wouldn't be here now if she had.

She replayed her afternoon with Triston and her departure from the inn in frustration.

No one but Luci and Ophelia would know her disappearance had anything to do with the duke…except maybe Triston. She had to trust he would figure things out and come for her.

This was all her fault. It was maddening. If no one came for her, Edith had no one to blame but herself. There was no one to save her but herself, but how could she figure out her own rescue when she had no idea where she was being taken or how far she'd need to go to escape and find help.

The carriage slowed and turned sharply, causing Edith to slide and her head to slam against the side of the box.

"Ouch!" She instinctively moved her hand to her head, but was unable to reach the spot.

The carriage moved slower down a heavily rutted path. Branches scraped the side of the conveyance as if they passed through what must be a wooded area.

After what seemed like another hour of being tossed about like a helpless ragdoll, they stopped. The carriage shifted as the driver disembarked.

It was time…her abductor—most likely Abercorn or his servant—would remove her now. The time had come to figure out her course for escape. Her heartbeat pounded in her ears as she attempted to listen for approaching footsteps.

Edith pushed back toward the large split in the wood but could not see much beyond what the pool of light from the lamp showed her. A flat grassy area with a sliver of a modest house almost out of view.

Now that the horses' hooves and carriage wheels had gone quiet, another sound could be heard.

She breathed in deeply, confirming that what she heard was correct—sure enough, the salt in the air was heavy with the breeze coming off the ocean. What she heard were waves slamming against a cliff.

She stilled for a moment when another thought struck her.

Abercorn had pushed Tilda down a flight of stairs with several witnesses within earshot *and* eyesight. There was nothing stopping him from pushing Edith off a cliff with no one the wiser. The duke was older than her father. Could she fight back and escape? Where would she go? From what she'd seen as they traveled after she woke, they hadn't passed any villages or journeyed through any towns. She may need to walk for hours before finding help, and there was always the chance Abercorn or his driver would locate her.

The carriage door opened, and the springs on the conveyance barely squeaked when someone alighted.

Suddenly, frigid air reached every inch of her skin as the lid of the boot was lifted.

A masked face came into view as Edith tried to look past the man to identify where they'd taken her, beyond it being a coastal area.

"Sit up, m'lady," an unfamiliar, gravelly voice commanded. "I be help'n ye out, but if'n ye try ta run or harm me, I'll havta club ye again." His eyes narrowed beneath his black mask. "Ye hear, or do I be need'n ta keep a close watch on ye?"

"I—I—I—" Edith worked to string together a coherent response. She did not want to be hit again, and she most certainly didn't want the man setting a hand on her. "I will not be any trouble...if only you will tell me why I'm here."

The man slipped a hand under her elbow and assisted her to the ground.

Edith stilled her body's natural response to pull away as revulsion overtook her.

In the several minutes it took to accomplish this feat with her hands bound, Edith noticed that a quaint cottage stood about a hundred feet from the carriage, yet she could not assess the house in detail because her eyes were drawn behind the building.

A sheer cliff dropped off another three hundred feet behind the cottage, the sea pounding relentlessly against the rocks as the waves splashed over and onto the area surrounding the house.

Her muscles tensed, and a scream ripped from her

throat. Her captor snarled, cutting off her yell as she gasped for breath.

"Scream again, and I be forced ta cut yer tongue from yer mouth." The man pulled the hood back over her head with a sharp tug, throwing her into complete darkness once more. But unlike before, Edith knew what surrounded her and where her fate lie—at the rocky, sea-soaked bottom of a cliff.

Would her death be slower than Tilda's? Edith prayed the hand above took mercy on her and made her demise a swift one.

"Go on." The man grasped her elbow and steered her toward...she was uncertain, but she prayed it was the cottage and not the cliff.

She hadn't been given time to properly process her final moments: what she needed to think over, whom she would miss most, and who would worry about her. None of it truly mattered anyhow. She'd be gone—with little trace. She only prayed her friends, and her family, would not waste time searching for her because she would never be found at the bottom of a cliff. She'd be washed away within minutes.

Her stomach twisted at the thought of never seeing her parents again, leaving Luci and Ophelia wondering what had happened to her, and Triston...oh, blast it all, but she'd been affected by their kiss.

Her face moistened with shed tears. For once she was thankful for the hood that blocked her face from view as it soaked up the sign of her weakness.

Had this been Tilda's final thought? Had she worried that her loved ones' lives would be ruled by her death?

Edith walked as slowly as the man allowed, not ready to know her fate, and needing more time. She'd only, just that evening, had her first, proper kiss. It had been everything she'd imagined, though not with the type of man she'd always dreamed of.

Lord Torrington, Triston—she allowed herself a

moment to repeat his name in her mind. He was arrogant and demanding with a likeness far more alluring than any poet could capture with words. He was Adonis to her, a creature famed to exist, but one which no man had bared witness to except in the pages of books. His chiseled jawline and broad shoulders fell within the dictates of myth, while his extreme height, thick legs, and solid frame were more suited to a warlord of centuries past. His touch had been gentle despite his size. His words soothing despite his deep tone.

Her foot caught on something, and she almost tumbled to the ground, but the man held her arm tightly and yanked her back before she fell completely.

"Wait here an' don't ye move." Two knocks sounded, and Edith heard the door open. "Come on."

She was pulled into the room and pushed down onto a chair. It was far better than the boot; however, the room had a deep chill and musty odor, as if the hearth hadn't seen a fire in many years, and the floors hadn't been cleared of dirt and dust in far longer. The floorboards creaked as the man stood in front of her and untied her wrists. Instantly, Edith flexed and twisted her cramped hands, attempting to banish the numbness that had set in at some point in their journey.

Her freedom was short-lived, however, when he stepped behind her and snapped her arms behind the chair, tying them together there. The motion sent a jolt of pain from her bruised shoulder to her heart, increasing the throbbing to the point where colors once more danced before her closed eyelids.

Yet, relief flooded her. She'd been taken inside the cottage—a reprieve from death, at least for a short while.

"May I have something to drink?" Maybe if she kept the man talking, he would share something that would help her escape. Or, possibly, she could convince him to untie her and allow her to go free.

"M'lady." The man groaned as he walked across the room. "She be secured, an' won't be cause'n any trouble for ye. If ye be certain ye don't be need'n a fire, I will take me leave now."

Edith's head whipped from side to side, attempting to see through the hood over her head, but nothing was clear. She hadn't realized someone else was in the room. Edith hadn't detected any other movement or breathing; however, after the door had shut, she sat very still and listened more intently. The rustle of brocade, the tapping of a slipper on a wooden floor, and the smell of berries assaulted her.

Someone was in the room with her.

And it was a woman—not Abercorn, as Edith had anticipated.

There was no woman who had cause to harm Edith. An unexpected release of tension caused her to sag in the chair. This was a mistake, all of it a misunderstanding.

It was then Edith realized she'd planned to demand answers from the man before he did away with her. She needs must know, even if she were unable to pass on the information to Luci and Ophelia, if the duke was responsible for Tilda's fall.

Edith held her tongue, determined not to be the first to break the silence. She could think of no logical reason for someone to bash her over the head and steal her away from London.

"What is your purpose with Abercorn?" The woman's deep, sultry voice was calm, as if she were asking if Edith wanted cream in her afternoon tea or if she favored sheep's wool or fox hair lining her coats. "How about Triston, Lord Torrington? Why does he keep sniffing about your skirts?"

Her relief was short-lived as a fresh wave of confusion and unease set her on edge. The rope keeping her hands bound cut into her skin when her body tensed.

Edith wracked her memories for a woman who had connection to both Abercorn and Triston, but the only two were Lady Prudence and Lady Chastity, and they were not the sort for mischief. Heavens, the pair rarely left the potted palms bordering ballrooms and shrank from view at other societal gatherings. They were most certainly not ones for kidnapping.

"What, do you not speak?" the woman purred.

A chair creaked, and Edith suspected her captor was coming toward her.

She pulled at her bound arms once more, but her bonds were tight to the point of sending excruciating pain up her arms whenever she moved. Her mind bounced between thoughts of being outnumbered by the servant and this woman—or if a better chance at survival hinged on her remaining silent or giving the woman what she wanted so desperately she'd kidnap a woman for it. Certainly, Edith could find out what the woman wanted and give it to her. A simple, rational conversation would bring this all to an end and have her back in London before too much damage had been done.

"Do not think to escape, Lady Edith." The woman's calm, cultured tone turned to a hiss. "I have no reservations about harming you."

"What do you want?" Edith's voice was muffled by the hood, but the woman's cold laugh said she'd detected Edith's renewed terror. "Lord Abercorn was married to my friend, and Lord Torrington and I are merely acquaintances."

"Abercorn is not wed to your friend now," she stated, her footsteps growing close—slow and deliberate. "But, still, you were meddling about his property a fortnight ago."

Edith wanted to demand how the woman knew any of this.

"And I saw you keeping watch over both Abercorn and Triston at the Gunther's ball." Her captor's footsteps halted, and Edith felt the woman's breath upon her cheek.

She wanted to deny her interest in Triston at the Gunther's ball. It was Abercorn—and Triston's sisters' safety—she'd been concerned with. While she'd been keeping a close eye on Abercorn, this woman had been watching *her*, along with Luci and Ophelia. Were they safe? Had they been taken, as well?

"And then you followed Triston from Hyde Park. Now, this does not appear to me to be the actions of mere acquaintances. Is my thinking faulty, Lady Edith?"

She flinched back at the woman's seething rage.

CHAPTER 13

"OPEN THE BLOODY door, Abercorn, you scoundrel!" Triston released another volley of fist pounds on the duke's townhouse door, the journal still clenched tightly in his other hand. He should have heeded Edith's warning about the man. He should have listened. He should have confronted Abercorn before now. "Open up before I tear this door from its hinges!"

"Mayhap he is not home?" Lady Ophelia whispered.

Triston turned sharply, immediately regretting his scowl when the woman flinched back as if burned.

Abercorn had to be home.

Edith had to be inside. This fiasco had to end now—this night—before anyone became the wiser about her disappearance. He pictured her the day they'd met, the sun reflecting off her golden crown as if she wore the halo of an angel—the image quickly transformed into Edith, hunch in a corner, stark terror etching her face as tears streamed down, falling one by one to the ground at her feet.

His temper flared red hot.

Triston took a step back, preparing to kick the latched door when hurried footsteps sounded from inside. The bolt was thrown, and the door pulled back a crack. No light shone from the dark foyer beyond.

The Abercorn butler's familiar face peeked out at Triston. "Lord Torrington? My master is out and is not expected until the morrow."

"Where is he?" Lucianna demanded from over Triston's shoulder.

"He has been at Lord and Lady Frampton's house party since yesterday." The man pulled the door open farther, his alarm subsiding. "Is there something I can do for you?"

"You are certain the duke is not home?" Ophelia asked timidly.

"I am quite certain, miss." The servant's head bobbed with his words.

"Very well. We will not bother you further." Triston pivoted and marched back toward his waiting carriage, the pair of ladies close behind. "Let us be off."

He waved his arm for the women to regain their seats in the carriage.

"Where will we look next?" Ophelia stared at him, her face blank. "I cannot think of anyone who would seek to harm Edith, except Lord Abercorn...if he knew we were watching him closely."

Something nagged at Triston. He flipped Edith's journal open, but there were no new scribblings since he'd looked through it earlier in the evening. Turning back to the pages filled with notes on Abercorn—notes Triston hadn't deemed important enough to read earlier—he scanned the page and Edith's hurried words until he located the day he'd met her.

The day she'd fallen from the tree.

The day he'd gotten a rather impromptu look at her undergarments.

He thought back to that day. Edith had stated clearly she hadn't been their snooping on him or his father, but Abercorn.

"Do you plan to sit here?" Lady Lucianna huffed, not bothering to truly look at the object he held. "We need to be searching for Edith, not sitting in your father's drive while you...read a book."

"It is Lady Edith's journal," he replied, not bothering to take his eyes off the page he scanned.

There it was. *Abercorn appears to be entertaining a very naked, raven-haired woman in the top, right, east-facing window.*

Triston leaned forward and stared up at the noted window. The drapes were firmly pulled, but he assumed the room to be Lord Abercorn's private quarters. Had this been what had startled her so greatly she'd tumbled from the tree?

He flipped to the final page about him—penned just that afternoon.

Lord Torrington is spotted with his sisters in the park, accompanied by the same dark-haired woman from Abercorn's top window(?).

Abercorn and Esmee?

Triston's heart plummeted to his feet. He was unaware the pair were familiar with one another, more than being passing acquaintances.

"M'lord!" Ames's call came from the shadows of the Downshire townhouse. "M'lord. You are here. I do not know what happened. I was follow'n the miss as ye instructed—"

He pivoted toward his manservant and glared toward the shadows he waited in, his eyes narrowing to see the man. "Ames. What happened?"

"Who is he?" Lady Lucianna leaned out the open window, her eyes also focusing on Ames as he stepped out of the shadows.

"M'lord, I be try'n ta tell ye." Ames cupped his shoulder, his other arm wrapped around his midsection. "I was follow'n the miss when she came ta ye father's home. I thought it be strange, but then I seen ye mother—pardon—stepmother, lurk'n about the drive. Her maid load'n her travel'n coach."

"Slow down. Breathe, my man or you are likely to expire before you can finish."

The man took several deep breaths, eyeing Lady Lucianna, his reservations clear.

"Now speak!" she demanded.

"While I be watch'n the marchioness, the miss be watch'n ye neighbor's home. Then someone bashed me across the back. I fell ta the ground, I did. That big rock over there"—he removed this hand from his shoulder long enough to point to the bounder placed close to Triston's father's townhouse—"I fell and hit that. Knocked me breath right out. When I gained me senses, m'lady, miss, and the coach be gone. Disappeared."

Without another thought, Triston called to his driver, "Southend-by-Sea! Lady Downshire's familial home on the cliffs. With haste!"

"Southend?" Lucianna's brow furrowed. "That is in East Essex, nearly a four-hour journey from here."

"Yes, it is. All the more reason we should hurry." Triston pulled the door closed and sat back. "They have a several-hour lead on us."

"*They* who, my lord?" Ophelia's breathless tone said she might be in danger of fainting. "I should send word to my father—"

"There is no time." Lucianna gave Ophelia a stern look.

"Very true." Triston nodded in agreement as the carriage started out of the drive.

"What will ye have me do'n?" Ames shouted over the moving carriage wheels as he hobbled alongside the conveyance.

"Follow us and stop in Hadleigh. Collect the magistrate and demand he come to the cliffs!" Triston sat back, confident his servant would not let him down. Next, he faced the two women across from him. Lady Lucianna had him pinned with her assessing, narrowed glare while Lady Ophelia sat wide-eyed and visibly shaking. "I will explain everything on the way, but we must be going."

His stepmother and former betrothed, Esmee, was

a callous, spiteful creature. But harming another, especially a woman? That did not seem within her at all. The act would not benefit her in any way, and if Triston knew anything about Esmee, it was she only did what benefited her. However, if Abercorn were with her— and they were embroiled in some sort of illicit *affair*— there was no deducing what the pair was up to.

Triston only hoped he and Edith's friends arrived in time. From the blood on the journal, he suspected that Edith had struggled with her abductor and had been injured in the process.

"We should not have pushed her to continue looking into Abercorn," Ophelia mused aloud, wringing her hands in her lap. "If anything happens to her, it is our fault. The duke is a dangerous man…we knew that, yet still we needed answers."

"Do not say this." Lucianna placed her arm around her friend's shoulders as they shook with a silent sob. "We were all doing our part to prove the man guilty of Tilda's death. Yet, mayhap we should have come together and not allowed her to spy on the duke alone."

"Do you truly think Abercorn is behind this?" Lucianna asked, pinning her glare on Triston as if he should have prevented all this.

Blast it all, he wished he'd been close enough to stop it.

"I am uncertain if Abercorn is solely involved, but we are headed for my stepmother's cottage. It was gifted to her on her sixteenth birthday by her maternal grandmother. It lays mostly unused. I, myself, have only been there once. It is a long journey, and I suggest the pair of you rest. We will arrive by sunrise."

The women stared out the window as they traveled beyond London and into the darkened countryside. The easy, well-oiled sway of the carriage may lull the women to sleep; however, Triston would get no rest until he knew for certain Edith was uninjured and back with her family—and with him.

His jaw clenched at the ludicrous notion. They'd shared *one* kiss—a rather innocent one, at that. There was little possibility he'd so much as crossed her mind after she departed his lodgings. Unfortunately, the same was not true for him. He'd thought of her while he bathed. He'd muddled his cravat more than once preparing for the soiree as he'd searched the room for her sun-kissed pale locks. If he'd hurried and arrived at the ball sooner, he would have discovered Edith's disappearance far earlier than he had.

Pushing the curtain from his window, Triston stared out at the night. A sea of darkness surrounded them with only the occasional glow of the moon through the overgrown trees bordering the rutted road.

He could not think what Esmee was doing consorting with Abercorn—if Edith's notes were correct, and the two dark-haired beauties were truly one and the same.

Hell, Triston had no doubt they were one and the same.

It was Esmee's way of things. She'd claimed an interest in him only long enough to catch his father's eye. She wed Lord Downshire quickly, securing her place as marchioness, but Abercorn could make her a duchess—did she not realize the messiness of divorce?

A part of him felt remorse for his father, duped by a woman he'd loved enough to hurt his own son to claim.

Triston wondered if he'd fought harder to keep Esmee if she'd have seen how much he'd truly cared for her—but, over time, he'd come to realize his attachment to the raven-haired woman was an emotion built solely on lust. It had never been anything close to love between them. He understood this now. The brief relationship he'd forged with Edith was far deeper than anything he'd experienced with Esmee. It only took Edith's disappearance to make him realize the depth of his connection to her.

His blood boiled at the thought of Esmee being responsible for what was happening to Lady Edith. He would journey to the far reaches of England to secure Edith's safety. He'd wage war against a fire-breathing dragon to make certain she was unharmed. And Triston would lay down his own life to make bloody certain Edith lived a life full of happiness and love.

Without a doubt, he was willing to give up his existence to secure hers.

A woman he'd met only a short time ago.

He didn't know her well enough to say if any of his feelings were love, and not more than any chivalrous gentleman would offer; however, he was driven to do far more for Edith than he had ever felt compelled to do for another person.

Triston was certain he could not look back. He could not turn away. He could not live his life as if Lady Edith had not completely taken over his every thought and action.

IT BECAME MORE and more difficult for Edith to draw breath through the thick hood, and her head still pounded while her shoulder and hip throbbed. Every one of her limbs was numb with cold. Intense shaking had overtaken her firm resolve to not show her panic to the woman who kept her bound.

Time was passing, and the servant hadn't returned, but then again, neither had she heard the carriage depart. At least there was someone still about with the power to stop this madness. Edith must speak with him, give him a reason to help her.

Was it morning yet? If her hood was removed would she see the sun had risen while she was tied to the chair?

And the woman currently stalking in front of her was nothing if not mad.

She moved from calm and reserved to angry and shouting to high-pitched laughter with a note of irrationality. The subject of the woman's inquiry seemed to bounce between topics just as rapidly as her temperament changed.

Despite several hours locked in the cold cottage with her, Edith was no closer to determining the woman's identity. She knew with certainty that she'd never heard her voice before. Was she a jilted lover of Abercorn's? Possibly another person the duke had harmed?

Edith was hard-pressed to keep her fear at bay long enough to concentrate on the mystery at hand.

"I am finding it difficult to breathe." Her voice was muffled and Edith was uncertain if the woman could understand her. "Can you please remove my hood?"

Edith had asked the same question several times before, but her captor never seemed to hear the question; instead moving on to another subject as if Edith hadn't spoken. It was as if the woman were wasting time—or waiting for someone to arrive. Everything was beyond Edith's comprehension. She was exhausted, her mind finding it hard to connect thoughts and words after so many hours bound to the stiff-backed chair.

"Mayhap a drink of water?" She attempted once more. "My throat is—"

"After all I have done, all I have suffered through, you and *Triston* think to ruin *me*?" Her voice cracked, and she laughed once more. "I cannot allow this to happen. Never will I allow this to happen. I have come so far, given up so much—I will not allow you, the spitting image of a porcelain doll with hair of pure gold and skin as fair as any English rose, and Triston to take from me what I have always deserved. A proper English rose, imagine that. Never would I have through Triston would favor such a dull chit."

The woman's words were becoming more and

more confusing as the hours passed and morning crept toward them. Edith could see muted light through her hood, something that hadn't been there before. The sun must be rising.

"I suppose it cannot hurt to remove your hood now," she mused, her feet starting again across the room. "He will be here soon. There are many things Triston is, however, lacking intellect is not one of them. Though I am far more clever than the pair of you. He will find your little notebook and come for you. If he needs any further proof, my maid let slip to the butler where I was going. I will have my confirmation that the pair of you will not cause my downfall."

"I can tell you, I have no idea what you speak of. You can set me loose now, and I will never say a word of this to anyone," Edith begged. "This must be some mistake or misunderstanding."

The hood was jerked from her head, the woman's grasp taking with it a thick lock of Edith's hair.

"Ouch!" Edith blinked rapidly to clear her blurred vision as she turned her head back and forth, taking in the room around her. However, the woman was nowhere to be seen.

"Look all you want," the woman hissed in Edith's ear. "Soon enough, you will see nothing but the watery cliffs below."

Her fears confirmed, Edith whipped her head sharply. The woman—the raven-haired beauty from Lord Abercorn's upstairs' window and Lord Torrington's carriage in Hyde Park—stood behind Edith, her long locks tumbling down over her shoulders in disarray, her icy-blue eyes widened in madness.

This must be the woman Triston spoke of, the one who had betrayed him for his own father. "Lady Downshire." Breathlessly, Edith turned away from the lady to hide her utter shock. A window stood directly before her. The carriage that had brought her sat in the drive, the driver now leaned against the side, his mask discarded during the night. "Please, allow me to leave. I will never speak to Lord Torrington again. I will stay far from Abercorn and his properties. You will never see me again."

"Oh, very shortly I will never have cause to see you or Triston again," Lady Downshire cackled. "Mayhap I should be rid of you now? I can't have Triston being the hero and embarking on the folly of saving you."

She needs must keep the woman talking, must stall her. "Do you truly expect Lord Torrington to come for me?" Edith asked, keeping her eyes trained out the window, silently begging the servant to come to her rescue, but he never glanced in her direction. "I am barely acquainted with him. He has no reason to worry about me."

Lady Downshire moved into her line of sight, her hands clasped behind her back. For the first time, Edith gained a clear view of the woman. Young, but her face held deep lines. She could not be more than a few years Edith's senior. The woman's deep hair, unblemished skin, and catlike eyes were alluring in a sensual way. She understood what had drawn Triston to this woman; she was captivating in her exotic appearance.

But why hadn't *he* been enough for her?

"You were betrothed to Lord Torrington?" It was as good a subject as any, and hopefully, one that would keep the woman talking until Edith could discern a means for escape. "I am sorry things did not go as planned."

Lady Downshire's hands fell to her sides, and a sneer settled on her face, marring her lovely features as rage overtook her. "Do not speak as if you know anything. You are a senseless maid with no knowledge of life."

"I assure you, I know much of life…and loss." Edith lowered her eyes to her lap, not wanting Lady Downshire to see how much it hurt her to admit anything about Tilda's death, especially to a woman obviously intimately connected to the man she feared had played a part in her friend's demise. "You can talk to me."

Without warning, the woman lashed out, her flat palm landing against Edith's cheek with a crack. Her neck whipped sharply and heat boomed across Edith's face. She pressed her lips together, determined not to cry out from the pain and shock of the woman's venom.

She turned away from Edith, moving without further word to a chair across the room. It must be the place she'd sat silently when Edith and been brought into the cottage.

Thankfully, Lady Downshire's anger seemed to ebb as she sank into the chair, her shoulders sagging as her scowl relaxed to a mere frown, her thoughts obviously drifting to another time and place.

Edith stared back toward the window, a cloud of dust could be seen in the distance.

Her heart sped up. Someone was coming.

The approaching carriage remained unnoticed by the driver leaning against Lady Downshire's coach as he stared off toward the cliffs beyond the cottage.

The roar and slap of the waves likely drowned out the sound of the coach and four horses.

"Ah, it must be him," the woman sighed pulling back the cloth and staring out the window. "It is indeed. Triston has finally arrived. You know, I thought he would arrive hours ago. Is it possible he does not care for you as much as he cared for me?"

CHAPTER 14

"LOOK!" OPHELIA EXCLAIMED, her nose pressed firmly to the windowpane, keeping out the early morning ocean breeze. "There is a carriage. She must be here."

After long hours of pondering the situation, Triston was certain Edith would be found within the cottage at the end of the drive. His father's carriage waited out front, but no sign of the Abercorn coach could be seen. His elation was only dimmed by his cautious nature—and the need to get his hands on Esmee and demand she give him answers.

The morning fog off the cold North Sea rolled in from the open waters to settle on the cliffs, only burning off once the midday sun crested above the area. If he'd journeyed here under any other circumstances, Triston would halt the carriage and take in the sight from the drive, a bit above the cottage and cliffs below.

Not today. Not ever would he gaze upon a cliff so majestic and not think solely of destruction and chaos.

And loss.

Esmee had taken Edith. There were no more lingering doubts once he spotted his family carriage outside of his stepmother's family home.

He stilled himself from throwing the conveyance

door wide and running the remaining way to the cottage. Triston could outrun the horses, his blood pumping violently through him would push him fast. However, he would not alarm the women across from him before it was necessary. If he raised their nervousness, they could very well find themselves in harm's way. They could not follow him into the cottage. He needed them to wait in the carriage until he'd determined Esmee was no threat and Abercorn wasn't also within the dwelling. He could not rescue Edith while keeping the other two women safe and out of trouble.

If he hadn't been so overcome with the need to find Edith, he would have realized sooner that the pair would have been safer remaining in London and allowing Triston to find and return Edith.

"I must ask a favor, Lady Lucianna." Triston looked to Edith's tall, slender friend—undoubtedly the leader of the group if her command of the situation during Edith's disappearance was any proof—for support. "I need you both to wait in the carriage while I enter the cottage."

"You think we should trust you?" Unease laced the woman's words as she assessed him.

Triston held his hands out, palms up. "I have brought you both this far. I care deeply for Edith's safety, as much as the pair of you." He moved to Lady Ophelia, her pensive expression meaning she was seriously thinking through everything. Maybe he should have addressed her first. "Lady Ophelia, it is imperative I keep all three of you safe—return you home whole and unharmed."

"You were incapable of completing that task when it was only Edith you were charged with. What makes you think we trust you to be able to step up with all three of us hanging in the balance?" Lucianna questioned.

Ophelia set her hand on Lucianna's arm. "Come

now, Luci. Lord Torrington has been honest with us thus far since discovering Edith's journal. We have little idea what we will find in the cottage. Let us allow him to venture in first."

Their carriage pulled up alongside his father's, with Samson leaning against it, his gaze on the cliffs beyond. The servant's family had been in the Downshire employ for three generations.

Triston bounded from the carriage before either woman had confirmed they'd remain out of sight. He needs must make sure they had some semblance of surprise—if Esmee hadn't already seen them. Walking around his father's coach, he immediately had Samson by the collar and twisted, cutting off the man's yelp before it left his throat.

"What have you done?" Triston hissed, bringing the servant's face close to his own.

"Lord Torrington!" Samson croaked, pushing at Triston to release him. "I—this—ye must—" he stammered.

"I *must* do nothing but allow the magistrate to deal with your misdeeds." Triston pushed the servant away, the sudden action sending the man splaying into the dirt. "Is it only Esmee and Lady Edith inside?"

When Samson remained silent, pushing himself back and away, Triston stalked forward. "If one hair on Lady Edith's head is harmed, it will not end well for you or Esmee, I swear to you."

"I—I—I never harmed the girl, m'lord. Swear on me pa, I didna." Samson crawled backwards. "I was only do'n what m'lady said."

"Kidnapping an innocent woman?" Triston seethed, advancing on the man. "Was it you who hit her? There was blood on her journal." Triston bit back the urge to pounce on the man, take out his pent-up aggression that had built during the four-hour journey to the sea.

"I startled the girl, and she bumped her head on a

tree branch. That be all, m'lord."

"What is Esmee's plan with her?"

"She doona be tell'n me much, but I heard her talk'n ta herself—she planned ta lure ye here." Samson tripped over himself, and he rushed to get the words out. "After that, I not be know'n. I swear ta it."

The woman was using Edith as a pawn to lure him to these cliffs.

Triston's lip curled back in a snarl, and his eyes narrowed one final time on the servant before he turned and called for his own driver. When he hurried over, Triston bit out each word as if it were his fist slamming into something—or someone. "Tie him up. Make certain he does not slip away. Ames should be here with the magistrate before long."

"Of course, my lord." The coachman ran back to the carriage and collected a length of rope from beneath his perch.

"You are not to give anyone anymore problems, Samson," Triston seethed. He didn't have time to deal with the disloyal servant. He needed to help Edith. "Do we have an understanding?"

Samson shook his head vehemently, spittle flying from his gaping mouth.

"Good, now give your hands to my driver," Triston demanded.

He barely paused to watch the coachman secure Samson's wrists.

"What is going on?" Lady Lucianna called from his carriage.

"Who is that man?" Lady Ophelia chimed in.

But Triston was already stalking toward the cottage, the cliffs surrounding it on three sides as the morning ocean spray relentlessly hammered the sheer rocks. He was uncertain if it was the din of the waves or the sound of his own blood thrumming through his veins that echoed in his head, blocking out all other noise.

His steps faltered when the silhouette of a woman

passed the large window—a pocket pistol held in her hands.

The tousled midnight hair and hurried, frantic movements did not fit the Esmee Triston knew. Something had broken loose within the woman, sending her into a manic spiral. He wracked his brain, attempting to remember any specific thing—either said or done—that would send Lady Downshire into such a maddened state.

His heart dropped as he looked closer. Edith was bound to a chair, her eyes widened in terror as Esmee advanced on her, the pistol pointed squarely at Edith—the rising sun gleaming off the pearl handle.

Triston moved in slow motion, his body not responding as quickly as he demanded…his breath heaving as he raced to stop Esmee.

The door to the cottage stood ajar, and Esmee's deep, throaty voice drifted toward him, halting his movement.

"…you see, I am to have a baby—the next Marquis of Downshire. My dear husband, Horace, is so deeply excited for our babe."

"Lord Torrington is to be the next marquis," Edith challenged.

"Correction, my dear Lady Edith, for I can see you are a bit daft," Esmee laughed. "Our poor Lord Torrington, my beloved stepson, will fall to his death this day. You see, he will be overcome by grief when he learns I am with child. He is still desperately in love with me. Everyone knows this to be true, even though I chose his father. He cannot handle I am to give birth to another Neville heir."

Triston lifted his foot to kick in the door, ready to remove the pistol from Esmee's hands and untie Edith, but her words halted him.

"And how do you know the child belongs to Lord Downshire and not Abercorn?" Edith's words were laced with conviction.

His pride—and affection—for Edith grew. She'd discovered Esmee's treachery when Triston, and his father, hadn't noticed anything amiss. His stepmother not only sought to dupe his father, but also do away with him to make way for her own child to inherit the Downshire estate. And there was no proof the child even belonged to the marquis' bloodline.

The woman was sadly mistaken if she thought he was so easy to be rid of.

"With you and Triston out of the way, no proof will exist to the contrary." Esmee waved the tiny pistol about.

Triston leaned close and peered through the crack in the door.

Esmee lowered the weapon and paced back toward the hearth. The tiny shot certainly wouldn't kill Edith from any distance, but up close, the pistol could cause serious injury. Especially if Esmee's aim were true.

"What of Abercorn," Edith asked. "Will he not suspect the babe is his?"

The woman threw her head back and cackled, it was the only way he could describe the sound, as if Edith had said the most insane thing.

His hair stood on end, and a shiver ran down his spine at the sound—so cold and emotionless.

"Enough." Esmee sobered, lifting the pistol once more and pivoting back toward Edith. Crossing the five paces to stand before her, she shoved the weapon in Edith's face. "You will keep your mouth shut!"

Triston noted that her hand shook, and the pistol wavered slightly.

He needed to end this charade.

Glancing over his shoulder, Triston saw Lucianna and Ophelia staring at him from the safety of the carriage.

Bloody hell, what had possessed him to travel without a weapon of his own? He clenched his jaw. Regardless, Esmee should not be hard to overpower.

Taking a final deep breath, Triston pushed through the door.

CHAPTER 15

EDITH SHRIEKED AT the same time Esmee turned sharply toward the door as it slammed against its frame. The shiny pistol slid from her grip and clattered along the floor until it hit the far wall.

Triston. Relief flooded Edith when he finally entered the cottage.

Both he and Lady Downshire followed the weapon's progress across the room, and Edith sighed, comforted to know the woman no longer held the gun.

Both Triston and Lady Downshire took off after the pistol; the woman scurrying across the room on her hands and knees, attempting to arrive at the far wall first, but Triston was quicker. He took hold of the weapon and held it high, out of the woman's reach, and she clawed at him and pulled on his shoulders to bring it back down. A deep sense of compassion welled inside Edith to notice that Triston did not aim the pistol at Lady Downshire, but only sought to keep it from her.

"Enough!" Triston commanded, his tone filled with power and leaving no room for argument; however, Lady Downshire seemed undeterred—and out of control—continuing to beat at Triston's chest.

Edith could not take her eyes off Triston—his hulking presence overtaking the room, commanding all present to heed his fury. His intense stare took her in next, from the obvious knot on her forehead, which ached with a fierce intensity that matched his stare, to her bound wrists, her uncontrollable shaking, and finally, coming to rest on her petrified gaze.

She knew exactly how she appeared—Edith had had a few opportunities to taken in her reflection in the window before her. She knew her hair was knotted, a twig tangled in her golden tresses. Her face was smudged with dirt from the carriage boot. And worst of all, her journal was gone, her hidden pocket ripped at the seams. Lady Downshire said she'd left it in London—odd to be concerned with a silly journal in such a terrifying moment.

Finally, Esmee stepped away, her heel catching on her gown, sending the woman tumbling, her arms pinwheeling and grasping for anything to stop her fall.

Edith watched as the woman's mouth opened in a silent scream as her head hit the table and she crumpled to the floor.

"Are you well, Edith? Tell me if you are injured." Triston set the pistol down and rushed to her side, reaching behind her to untie her wrists. "If she so much as—" He breathed.

"I am as well as can be expected after spending several hours in a carriage boot and many more tied to this chair, but nothing that will not heal with time and rest." Edith flexed her wrists, bringing them before her as Triston gently massaged the indentations from the rope. Feeling and warmth quickly returned to her fingers. "I shouldn't have been so foolish as to journey back to Abercorn's before going home…"

Triston placed a quick kiss to her lips, his heat banishing her chill.

"As heartwarming as this is, I will need to ask you to step away from Lady Edith, Triston," Esmee purred, rubbing the side of her head.

Glancing over his shoulder, she saw the woman

had collected her pocket pistol and held it aloft once more; however, this time, her hand was steady, and her gaze alight with a fury so deep, her icy blue eyes glowed in the dim cottage.

"Triston!" Edith couldn't say anything more before he flipped around.

As Edith stood, he pushed her behind him. "Go, Edith," he whispered. "Out the door, now!"

She didn't want to leave him, couldn't imagine fleeing and letting him get hurt—or worse yet, killed—because she wasn't here to help.

Her gaze assessed the room, looking for anything she could use as a weapon.

Triston slowly advanced on Lady Downshire. "Esmee, put the pistol down. You do not need to do this. It is over. Do not give me reason to restrain you."

"I am with child, you brute," the woman wailed, swinging the gun wildly at Triston. "You stay back from me. Your father will never forgive you if he learns you assaulted me in my delicate condition."

Triston sidestepped, attempting to keep one step ahead of her as she swung her pistol and he moved in a circle, leading the woman away from Edith. She knew the wise thing would be to hurry to the carriage as she'd been told, but her desire to remain and help Triston would not allow her to depart. It was her fault he was in danger in the first place. If she hadn't gone to Abercorn's townhouse again, if she hadn't followed Triston from the park—heaven help her, if she hadn't climbed into the tree all those weeks ago—he would have never been dragged into any of this.

And she never would have discovered how much she could care for a man. Her heart ached at the very thought of a life without him.

Lady Downshire would have continued her trysts with the duke, unbeknownst to her husband or Lord Torrington.

They would not currently be in the wilds of Essex

in a cottage overlooking sheer rock cliffs—a severe drop Esmee thought to cast both her and Triston over. All to save herself the embarrassment of being exposed as a lying, cheating adulteress, pregnant with another man's child.

The entire debacle was preposterous. Edith, and her friends had been in the business of collecting gossip and exposing the next scandal for almost a year now, but this was nothing Edith had ever wanted to be embroiled in.

Triston's Hessians scraped along the wooden floor, and he led Esmee away from Edith toward a door that opened in the kitchen.

Her pulse raced as she scrutinized the room one last time. The cottage was empty except for a lounge, table, chairs, and a few tarp-covered objects. Not so much as a fire poker to grasp if the need arose. It'd been too dark outside when she'd been let out of the carriage boot and her hood replaced before entering the cottage. There had to be something to use as a weapon outside. Maybe an ax to chop firewood or a long piece of wood…anything.

Triston was backing up through the door into the kitchen area with Esmee following, her pistol trained on Triston's heart.

If Edith hurried, she could find her own weapon and return within moments.

Edith followed Triston's lead and began backing up toward the front door which remained open, but kept a watch on Lady Downshire. The woman was mad enough to change course before either Triston or Edith suspected her switch in target.

Suddenly, an arm wrapped around her neck, and a voice hissed, "Where do ye think ye be makin' off ta?"

The servant's stale breath assaulted her neck, hot and sour.

Why hadn't she thought about what had become of the man who'd brought her in from the carriage?

Edith begged herself to remain still, to not say a word to distract Triston from his target. The servant began to pull her from the cottage and out toward the cliffs beyond, her feet coming out from beneath her as she tried to gain purchase. His free hand snaked around her waist, firmly pulling her to his body to cut off her struggles.

Glancing around the yard, she saw another man lying unmoving on the ground. Edith would never forgive herself if she were the cause of anyone else being injured.

Within a moment's time, they were around the house, and the prone man was blocked from her view by the cottage. The violent thrashing of the waves against the cliffs made it impossible for any screams to be heard. At least if she kept the carriage driver occupied, it was only Lady Downshire whom Triston need overtake before coming for her.

All hope was not lost.

Edith trusted Triston—he came for her even after learning she'd been spying on him.

Blast it all, she more than trusted him.

He would come for her again; she only need slow the driver down.

"Do not do this," Edith said, the man's arm tightening around her throat. "You will lose everything. And for what? That senseless woman inside the cottage?"

"Shut ye mouth!" He pulled up with the arm around her midsection, lifting her feet off the ground and moving faster toward the cliffs, no longer pulling but carrying her. "M'lady has never been senseless, ye best bet. She be a wondrous lady—who not a single soul appreciates. Not her husband, nor that nob Abercorn."

"You are in love with her," Edith croaked, her windpipe slowly crushing under the servant's tight hold. It wasn't a question...there was no other way to explain why a man would throw away his life to help a woman who'd kidnapped an innocent woman and lured a gentleman—a master within his household—to his death. "She does not love you."

Edith needs must make the man see reason. Lady Downshire loved nothing but herself and the status that came from marrying a wealthy, titled man.

"As soon as you do as she says, she is going to leave you—blame everything on you. You will be the one locked away at Newgate or hung for your crimes. Not her. She will return to London and live as if nothing happened." At her words, he tightened his grip even more, cutting off Edith's air and sending her head swimming.

"You, there!"

Edith's mind cleared instantly when Luci's voice thundered from behind them, causing the man to speed up.

"Duck!" Ophelia shouted.

Edith didn't need any more encouragement. She whipped from the man's hold and fell to the ground, rolling to the side and away from the cliffs.

There was no time to ponder how Luci and Ophelia had gotten all the way to Essex or even knew she'd been taken.

Thwack.

Edith turned and attempted to push herself to stand. Her friends were immediately at her sides with Ophelia grasping her elbow to help her stand. From the corner of her eye, Edith watched Luci throw a long piece of wood to the ground before nudging the servant with her slippered toe.

Luci turned back to Edith with a shrug when the man didn't move. "I guess he wasn't expecting that."

Edith's chest burned, and she sucked down a large gulp of air before doubling over in a coughing fit. The pounding in her head intensified once more, and her throat ached.

"How—I mean when—I cannot—"

"Shhhh." Ophelia rubbed her goose pimple-covered arms. "You are freezing. Let me get you back to Lord Torrington's carriage. There is a wrap waiting for you."

"Lord Torrington! Have you seen him?" Edith pulled from Ophelia's hold and started back toward the cottage. "Lady Downshire had a pistol trained on him. We must stop her!"

Luci bent to retrieve the wooden branch she'd hit the servant over the head with, but Edith shook her head.

"She is with child. We cannot harm her, or the babe might be injured, as well."

"But she kidnapped you." Luci's words were laced with disbelief. "How can you feel any sympathy for this woman?"

Edith hadn't contemplated her feelings for Lady Downshire; honestly, she only knew her for this one action. Though it was deplorable, she longed to know the many actions that came before it to bring the woman to such a place where she sought to harm a woman she'd never met—or Lord Torrington.

"It is not sympathy, Luci, but a sense any of us could have ended up in a similar position." Edith turned back toward the cottage as a set of double doors on the back side of the house were flung open, though the never-ending slap of the waves covered any sound. "We can discuss this later. We need to help Triston."

The women shared a knowing look, but Edith didn't pause long enough to question it.

Triston was slowly backing toward the cliffs with Lady Downshire in pursuit—her hands steadily holding the pistol. He didn't allow his eyes to stray toward Edith or her friends, though by the way his shoulders tensed, he'd seen them.

If they didn't act quickly, Triston would be forced over the cliff—taking Edith's hope for the future with him.

Waving to Luci and Ophelia, the trio sidled close to the cottage wall and followed it until they were directly behind Esmee, who pressed forward toward the cliffs at a slow pace.

Edith couldn't imagine the horrible, senseless, and hurtful words the woman spouted.

Lady Downshire's voice was swallowed by the increasing wind, only heard by her and Triston.

EDITH, WITH LUCIANNA and Ophelia close behind, edged their way along the cottage wall until they were directly behind Esmee. He was torn between pride at their bravado and a desire to shout at them to save themselves. Triston could not comprehend how Esmee hadn't noticed the trio or Samson lying prone on the ground only fifty feet away.

She'd always had a one-track mind, focused on the thing she wanted at that precise moment. It had been winning him once upon a time, but it had quickly changed to snaring a marquis—Triston's father—and eventually, having her own family. Odd he hadn't realized how much she'd changed over the years. She'd been willing to bed another man to make certain she carried a child as soon as possible, but Triston doubted she'd slaked her lust only with Abercorn.

Had Samson fallen prey to Esmee's viperous ways?

If Triston hadn't been able to resist the woman's treacherous charms, there was little possibility a mere coachman would turn away if his mistress took an interest in him. The depth of her manipulation sickened him. He felt an immense sense of pity for Samson, though that did not overshadow his part in Edith's disappearance.

"Esmee." He held his hands out, not wanting to incite her further. "Let us return to the cottage and discuss this. I am certain things are not as dire as you suspect."

He'd kept up the pretense that what had been said before he'd entered the cottage was still unknown to him. She thought him still pining away for her, continuing to miss what they'd briefly shared two years prior. No lit candle was held for the woman before him—it had been snuffed out the moment he'd caught his father in a compromising situation with Esmee in his study.

Shaking his head, Triston had to concentrate on the present, not the wounds from his past. They had healed, but if Esmee pulled the trigger on her pistol or caused him to fall from the cliffs, it would be the end of him...and Edith.

"Did you think I wouldn't find out what you and your little strumpet were up to?" Esmee waved her weapon before her, her grip so tight her knuckles were white. "There is no more time for talking, and I will not allow you to alter my course. The decision has been made."

The term *strumpet* incited Triston once more. Esmee, the woman who's easily betrayed him and his father thought to use such a word when speaking of Lady Edith?

She'd been seamlessly altering from composed to livid to a babbling mess making little sense. It had always been Triston's belief Esmee was a determined, persistent lady. She knew what she wanted, and she went for it. The woman stalking him toward the cliff's edge was not that woman.

"You do not need to do this, Esmee," he shouted to be heard above the growing noise of the waves at his back. "Lady Edith and I—"

"Are trying to destroy me!" Her eyes grew wide with madness. "I will not allow it. I am Lady Downshire, a marchioness. I will give my husband an heir."

"But he *has* an heir."

"*You?*" Spittle flew, and Esmee threw her head back in laughter. "My son will be the next Marquis of Downshire, not you, Triston."

"You plan to kill me?"

"Oh, no. You will jump from the cliff willingly." Esmee halted, her lips curling into the innocent smile Triston remembered from years prior. "You will be so distraught over the news of my pregnancy. You brought me here to declare your love, you see, but I rebuffed your advances. In the end, you could not handle the rejection, and unrequited love made you take your own life." She shrugged as if she'd painstakingly planned the entire situation and now only needed him to be the honorable gentleman and do as she said.

Did she think him the sort of man to beg, either for his life or for her love?

His chest tightened. He hadn't fought or begged for Esmee before or now, but he would for Edith. He needed her, and she needed him. For that to happen, he must be alive.

"Now, can we not get this over with?" she asked. "When I am done with you, I still have need to deal with your ladybird; though I am certain Samson has her occupied at the moment."

Triston focused on Esmee, not wanting his eyes to stray toward Edith and her friends, who were currently whispering amongst themselves. He only prayed the trio did nothing foolish to put them at risk. A wish he had a dreadful feeling would not go without frustration as the ladies had already proven themselves reckless.

Out of the corner of his eye, Triston saw Samson starting to regain his wits, though he hadn't managed a sitting position as yet.

If the servant were able to rejoin Esmee in her endeavors, the odds would be less in Triston's favor. He couldn't allow this to happen.

Bloody hell, Triston should have insisted his father make the journey with him, but there hadn't been time to convince the marquis. Belatedly, Triston hadn't even thought of the idea until London was far in their wake. The marquis would be hard-pressed to think his beloved wife capable of any of this.

Triston took another small step back, the overspray from the cliffs hitting the back of his neck and saturating his jacket. The lip of the sheer drop could only be a few paces away...and he was no closer to getting Esmee to see reason.

Edith and her friends fanned out behind his stepmother, moving slowly into a semi-circle of sorts as they blocked her in. They surrounded her on three sides with Triston taking the fourth position.

He shook his head slightly, hoping they'd see his silent plea and find their own safety.

Instead, the women only moved closer, trapping Esmee but also putting each of them at a greater risk of being the woman's new target.

Edith had taken the position directly behind Esmee—in Triston's line of view.

He took in the sight of her. Edith commanded all of his attention, holding him hostage. If these were his last moments, he would perish happily, knowing the images of Edith would be forever burned into his memory.

The woman was beautiful, her appearance nothing but sunshine and brightness with her delicate skin, sun-kissed, pale locks, and honey eyes.

He was helpless to do anything but watch as the trio shared a nod and all shouted in unison, their voices carrying high above the din of the ocean behind him, and echoing around them.

Esmee halted her advance, her head twisting this way and that to find out where the noise had come from. Her hand clutching the pistol dipped to her side, and Triston took the opportunity to pounce into action.

Triston leapt forward and took hold of Esmee's hand, wrenching the weapon from her.

Lucianna and Ophelia quickly stepped forward and grasped each of Esmee's arms.

Esmee's eyes widened in utter shock as she looked from one woman holding her to the other and desperately tried to tug herself free. A long, black strand of hair fell over her eyes, and Triston reached forward to brush it aside.

"It is over, Esmee," he sighed, uncertain if she heard him over the crashing waves. "There is no use struggling."

Esmee crumpled to the ground, the two women struggling to keep her from completely falling.

A deep, wrenching sob escaped her as her head fell forward and her damp, raven hair veiled her face from sight. Her shoulders shook, and her body trembled.

Edith stepped forward and knelt next to the woman who'd had such nefarious plans for her, and laid her arm around Esmee's heaving shoulders, leaning in close to whisper something in his stepmother's ear.

When Esmee nodded, Edith slipped her arm around the woman's back and helped her to stand.

Triston would have gladly taken Edith in his arms and walked away, but here she was, helping the woman who'd only an hour ago intended to push her off a cliff.

His heart swelled, and the despair of the previous night dissipated.

Edith led Esmee back toward the cottage with Lady Lucianna and Ophelia close behind. Her compassion for his stepmother baffled him. How could Edith want to be anywhere near Esmee?

When the group disappeared into the cottage, Triston turned toward Samson, but the servant was being led away by Triston's coachman.

His carriage still waited in the drive, but another plume of dust traveled toward him, another carriage approaching. It must be Ames with the Hadleigh Magistrate.

Bringing his arm to shield the sun from his eyes,

Triston watched the coach's harried approach with its four large, spotted horses pulling at the reins.

"My lord?" He turned away from the approaching carriage to see that Edith had returned to his side. "You must be cold. Luci is starting a fire inside. I think you should warm yourself."

"You always think first of others." He turned to her, tucking a lock of hair behind her ear before leaning down to kiss her forehead.

Edith pulled back and stared up at him, her brow furrowed. "It is what I have always been taught. If I put others first, my happiness will naturally follow."

Triston remained silent, running his thumb along her hairline where a large lump was forming. She was so innocent and pure—and because of him, that was shattered. He stared into her eyes, waiting for the moment her innocence would disappear and be replaced by darkness. With that, Edith would turn away from him. She had no other option—she exposed scandal, she did not live it herself. Unfortunately, things were to become far more complicated, and the risk of society finding out grew more pressing as the carriage carrying Ames and the magistrate arrived.

He doubted her coming happiness would include him.

CHAPTER 16

EDITH HEARD, RATHER than saw, yet another carriage arrive at the tiny cottage on the cliffs. It was as if the sea had realized the danger had passed because the roar of the waves subsided, bringing an almost peaceful hum to the tiny yard in front of the cottage.

There was nothing Edith wanted more than this moment.

She'd thought only an hour before her time with Triston was forever at an end. The chance to tell him exactly how much she cared for him would be taken from her; however, here they stood.

Both whole and safe.

Which meant Edith would have plenty of time to express to Triston everything her heart held for him. Speaking of her heart, it raced as he continued to stare down at her, his look softening and holding a meaning she couldn't quiet decipher.

A mixture of sorrow...and what?

Esmee and her loyal servant were being held inside the cottage with no danger of escape or chance of harming anyone else.

There was no reason for sadness—or regret—which was what she saw in Triston's eyes.

They should celebrate.

Without giving herself time to change her mind, Edith stood on her tiptoes, but his face was still out of reach. She encircled his neck with her arms, feeling that the hair at his nape was still damp, but this did not stop Edith from drawing Triston down to her.

She peered into his eyes. "Thank you for coming for me."

"I—"

Her lips met his, silencing his reply. Edith would not be able to go on if he told her he'd come out of any other reason but love—for her. His warm lips banished the cold that had settled on her long before the morning sun had risen. As she'd sat tied to the chair, the hood over her head, Edith truly believed she'd be cold and overrun by shivers forevermore; however, when Triston's arms wrapped around her waist and pulled her close, she knew, without a doubt, she'd never feel the icy tendrils of cold run through her again.

"Triston!"

He pulled back with the call of his name and set Edith back on the ground. However, their brief kiss was enough to give her hope there would be more to come. If not today, then tomorrow, or the day after. She was not allowing Triston to go.

"Triston!" They both turned to see Triston's father running toward them, his arms outstretched as if he did not touch his son, hold him quickly, he may disappear. "You are safe. Where is Esmee?"

The man, so much like his son with his great height and strong jaw, stopped and placed his hands on Triston's shoulders.

Behind them, a haphazardly dressed man, likely the Hadleigh magistrate awoken from his slumber, and another man sauntered toward the open cottage door where Ophelia shouted for their attention.

"She is inside, Father," Triston confirmed, and his father relaxed, the strain of the long carriage ride draining from his shoulders. "She is unharmed, physically."

The marquis shook his head. "I do not understand…"

Edith wanted to take Triston's arm, give him someone to lean on when he told his father the damning truth, but to her surprise, it was he who stepped free of his father's hold and pulled Edith close once more.

"Esmee is not well. Her mind…it is addled." The sorrow returned to him, and Edith thought maybe this was what had weighed on him since his stepmother was thwarted. "She, with Samson's assistance, kidnapped Lady Edith and brought her here, thinking to lure me to my death. She says she is with child."

"It cannot be," Lord Downshire mumbled, looking over Triston's shoulder to the cottage. "I must go to her. Have a physician summoned. I cannot…I am sorry…it is too much…"

"Go to her, my lord," Edith whispered. "Having you near will calm her, I am certain."

The marquis looked down at her, as if noticing her for the first time, and his eyes widened.

"Lady Edith… I cannot tell you how sorry I am for all this—"

She held up her hand to stop him. "Do not worry over me, go to your Lady Downshire."

Edith suspected her dirty clothes, knotted hair, and the atrocious lump on her forehead made her appear far worse than she actually felt.

With a nod, and another pat to Triston's shoulder to confirm he was truly solid and well, the marquis dashed inside the cottage.

Edith remained quiet and still at Triston's side as he watched his father go.

"I cannot believe he came," Triston mumbled.

"He loves you. You are his son, after all." Edith was only privy to the one exchange Triston had shared with his father at his boarding house before she was taken. The man did not seem one to show his affection for his offspring, but the love was there. Edith was sure of it. "Shall we go inside and help?"

"Heavens no," Triston said, his hand caressing her cheek. "I think we have done our part for the day."

She held her breath, waiting for him to say more. When he didn't, Edith sighed. "I am sorry for causing you and your family so much trouble. If we hadn't been so fixated on Abercorn, none of this would have happened."

Triston leaned down and placed his lips to her forehead, being sure to keep away from the knot. "No, I should have heeded your warnings about the man."

"You do not think us foolish for our continued persistence with Abercorn?" She closed her eyes, concentrating on the feel of his mouth as it trailed from her forehead, to her cheek, to her jaw with an aching slowness until he reached her lips.

He kissed her right there, not caring who saw their intimate moment—and her question dissipated. It no longer mattered as he lifted her from the ground, and Edith ran her hand through his hair, pulling him ever closer to her.

CHAPTER 17

EDITH ALLOWED HER eyes to drift closed, the sway of the moving carriage tempting her to sleep, safely tucked against Triston's side. She was exhausted, yet it had taken nearly an hour for her nerves to settle enough for the tension to drain from her. Her head still ached, throbbing in time with her hip.

However, she was unharmed.

Both she and Triston were unscathed, while they'd left Lady Downshire in the care of her husband, the Hadleigh magistrate, and a local physician. Samson had confessed all—including his own tryst with his mistress. Edith despised watching the hurt in the marquis' eyes as he learned of his wife's treachery firsthand.

Esmee was a gently bred lady of the *ton*, married to a wealthy, influential lord.

Which meant, if Triston's father did not deem her actions worthy of punishment, then Lady Downshire could very well return to her place among society with impunity for her deeds.

She was obviously demented and in need of a physician's care, especially if she were with child. Seeing as how Triston's father—at Prudence's and Chastity's insistence—had accompanied Ames to Lady Downshire's home in Essex, she doubted the woman would continue as she had before—or planned to after doing away with Edith and Triston. At the very least, she'd be removed from London to the Downshire country estate, Carlton Curlieu Hall in Leicestershire, until after the babe was born. Triston had reassured her of this after handing her, Luci, and Ophelia into their carriage.

As they'd started back toward London, they'd each fallen into their own silent musings as the miles passed. Luci and Ophelia were tucked tightly under a woolen blanket on the opposite seat, while Edith had selected to sit beside Triston as opposed to between her friends.

Yet, neither woman seemed to judge her harshly for the choice.

Triston was ever so warm, giving her the heat she'd lacked after the cold night she suffered. He pulled her a bit closer at that moment, and Edith couldn't stop her smile.

Unexpectedly, his lips pressed to her forehead.

Edith couldn't prevent her sigh of contentment from escaping.

"We will be back in London before we know it," Triston mumbled to no one in particular.

"And how are we to explain our disappearance to our parents?" It was unnecessary for Edith to open her eyes to know Luci sat across from her, her arms crossed and a scowl on her face. "And arriving home in your carriage…we will all be ruined."

"Better ruined and alive than dead and forgotten at the bottom of a cliff," Ophelia chimed in.

Edith giggled at Ophelia's impertinent comment, knowing it would only further inflame Luci.

Her friend only huffed. Cracking her eyes, Edith watched as Luci turned to stare out the window, her arms—as suspected—crossed.

"Do not fear, ladies," Triston replied.

"We have everything to fear, Lord Torrington." Luci's cool demeanor broke wide. "We cannot trust you to fix all of this for us."

"Did I not tell you to have faith I would rescue Edith?"

"Yes," Luci reluctantly agreed. "But—"

"And did I not follow through on that promise?"

"Oh, my lord, you certainly did…with our assistance!" Ophelia exclaimed, tugging the blanket away from Luci to cover her own legs. "You were quite dashing and a regular white knight. You must admit, Lucianna, Lord Torrington did know where to find Edith, and he kept that madwoman distracted long enough for us to bash the poor coachman over the head."

Luci snorted. "I will admit nothing of the sort."

"Then I suppose I should direct my driver to head for Gretna Green." Triston shrugged.

Edith's shoulders straightened. There was only one reason for a person to travel to Gretna Green, and Edith could not entertain the very notion for fear it would lead to her disappointment.

"Gretna Green!" Ophelia sat up straight, her eyes as wide as tea saucers, mirroring Edith's own startled look. "Why would we journey to Scotland?"

"To avoid scandal—I will wed Lady Edith, and you two will be our witnesses." He spoke as if the idea weren't completely outlandish. "When we return to London, it will be as husband and wife, and you two will be properly chaperoned."

Husband and wife? Edith allowed the preposterous notion to settle within her. To have Triston by her side for all eternity? It seemed too much for her to hope for.

"You think a hasty marriage across the border will stall the gossips?" Luci narrowed her glare on him.

"If that does not stop any whisper of scandal, then I am certain the trio of you can say…" He tapped his chin in thought. "Have a letter posted in the *London Daily Gazette* to clarify the circumstances surrounding Edith's hasty marriage to a man more handsome than any lord in decades. You can also reassure your readers that though I am a sturdy man, I am not, in fact, as strong as an ox nor as arrogant as a London dandy."

"I believe I compared you to a Greek god—Adonis—not oxen." Edith leaned away from Triston and stared up into his molten cocoa eyes, his humor evident in his smirk.

"My dear Lady Edith, you still possess the skills of a snake with your lightning-quick ability to persuade." He pulled her close once more, this time, bringing his lips to hers.

Not caring that both of her friends gasped in surprise, Edith pushed herself ever closer to Triston, not daring to allow him room to pull away from her. She'd allowed him to send her away once, and they'd almost lost each other. It would not happen again.

"I suppose we do owe you our sincerest gratitude for assisting us in finding Edith; however, let us keep in mind she would not have been taken had it not been for you, Lord Torrington."

Edith released Triston's lips long enough to laugh. "That is the best you will get from Luci, my lord. I would take it as a 'thank you' and move on."

"I think I will take your advice." He brought his hands to cup her face, his thumb lightly grazing the spot where she'd been hit. "Oh, and I intend to have that blasted tree removed from my father's London drive."

"Just because you have proven yourself worthy, does not mean we will stop our pursuit of Lord Abercorn—and other men who think to cause women harm." Luci leaned back in her seat, tugging a portion of their wrap back from Ophelia.

"I cannot stop any of you from this course; however, I will caution you against writing any piece that is not solidly grounded in facts."

"You will not demand we stop?" Ophelia asked.

"Of course, not," Triston replied. "My dear sisters happen to enjoy the *Mayfair Confidential* column greatly. I will not be the cause of their displeasure. Now, I pose the question once more: where do we go from here? I can instruct my driver to London, or on to Scotland."

Edith's heart spiked as she waited for her friends' responses.

"You truly mean to wed Edith?" Luci asked, eyeing him closely.

Even Edith felt a measure of uncertainty under her friend's intense stare.

"If she will have me, yes. However, I prefer a more traditional approach than a Gretna Green wedding." He turned to Edith once more. "If you will have me, and your parents agree to our match, I would insist on a proper betrothal and a large wedding—as quickly as possible. Unless you prefer Gretna Green, that is."

Her heart fluttered once more, and Ophelia sighed dramatically.

"And what if my parents object?" She would not share with him that her parents would never object to a match Edith wanted. "What then?"

"It will be my turn to kidnap you!"

"Oh, Lord Torrington, I think you may have convinced me noble men exist, after all," Edith sighed. "And love is certainly possible."

"Love?" Luci hissed as if saying the very word burnt her tongue.

Edith pulled back and stared across the carriage at her dearest friends. "Yes, love. We must remember, no matter how much we long to discover what truly happened the night Tilda fell down those stairs, we cannot forget to find our own happiness. She would have wanted that for all of us, far more than spending our lives reliving her passing and never moving forward to secure our own futures."

"You expect me to easily forget that Abercorn caused the demise of our friend?" Luci asked. "To act as if it didn't happen and go on enjoying the endless soirees and nights at the opera, all while my heart is heavy and burdened?"

"We will never forget Tilda." Ophelia nodded.

Edith knew Ophelia risked Luci's wrath if she openly agreed with Edith.

"I am not asking you to forget—or stop keeping a close eye on Abercorn—however, we can also seek our own futures in the process." Edith needed her friends to understand that while they were all burdened with grief and guilt over Tilda's death, that did not mean their hearts should be closed off to finding their own paths in life. "Please, just consider the possibility that we can continue helping others remain free from the clutches of evil scoundrels, but also find our own peace with life."

"I will do everything in my power to help," Triston offered. "I will contact Bow Street and have Abercorn followed until we learn if he is responsible, or the trio of you are satisfied he poses no threat to others."

"That is very kind of you, but far too kind. We cannot put you at risk." Tears threatened to fall, but Edith held them back. "*We* have issue with Abercorn, not you. I cannot ask you spend your resources to help us."

Triston already lived in a boarding house under the weight of his father's generous allowance. She could not ask him to spend coin he did not possess; however, he would have rightful use of her dowry if they wed.

"Edith," he sighed. "I care very deeply for you— your well-being and that of Lady Lucianna and Lady Ophelia—therefore, I would not be an honorable man if I allowed you to continue without offering assistance. And because my sisters have set their sights on the trio of you. I promised no harm would come to any of you."

"It seems your life is full of domineering, undaunted women, determined to continue along their chosen paths, Lord Torrington," Ophelia offered with a laugh.

"I would have it no other way." He placed another

kiss on Edith's forehead. "But I will request something in return."

Luci's brow rose in question. "I assumed as much."

"I expect both of you to speak fondly of me to Lord and Lady Shaftesbury." He winked. "I have my own path in mind, and I am determined to bring Lady Edith along, as my wife."

EPILOGUE

London, England
February 1815

THE EVENING WAS exactly as Edith had always dreamed it would be: the musicians played each piece to perfection, the ballroom was decorated in lovely shades of pink and gold, the chandeliers above the crowded room glowed with light, and everyone was enjoying their evening of merriment, celebration, and revelry to honor Lady Edith Pelton's betrothal to Lord Torrington.

Especially the besotted groom and his wife-to-be, as they twirled about the dance floor.

Triston's hold was a bit too tight to be proper, but not so close their betrothal would commence with talk of scandal.

Besides, no one dared speak of any indecent activities if the *Mayfair Confidential* column had yet to comment on it. And the *London Daily Gazette*'s gossip column had advertently allowed slip that Lady Edith Pelton, with her dearest friends in tow, had suffered a devastating carriage accident on a darkened route outside London after they'd snuck from their homes for a midnight excursion. If the dashing Lord Torrington hadn't happened upon the stranded women, they likely would have been set upon by thieves or, worse yet, wild beasts. Furthermore, it was stated any other man would not have had the brute strength to lift the back of the carriage high enough for their driver to replace the broken wheel.

Ophelia had giggled openly as she'd written that portion of the column.

Thankfully, Edith had been present to see Triston roll his eyes heavenward and chuckle at the obvious mention of his immense proportions.

Even now, swirling around her family's townhouse ballroom, Edith felt tiny in his arms as he towered over her.

Imagine her parents' shock when Triston had asked for Edith's hand in marriage only a fortnight after their return from Essex—or as Lord and Lady Shaftesbury still believed—her night stranded alongside the dark road outside London.

"Your smile shines brighter than a million candles, my love," Triston whispered, pulling her to his side as the musicians played the final note. "Our lives will never know a moment of darkness as long as you are near."

"You are a shameless flirt, my lord." Edith smiled up at him, placing her hand upon his arm as they departed the dance floor and made their way toward Luci and Ophelia. "Whatever am I to do with such a man?"

"Keep him close at all times," he teased.

Edith and Triston both nodded a greeting to the Marquis of Downshire as they passed, Pru and Chastity keeping close to their father's side.

"Has his melancholy lessened?" Edith whispered, smiling at Triston's father as they moved on.

"I fear he may never recover from Esmee's betrayal. He loved her deeply, even though we all knew her to be flawed." Triston slowed his pace. "However, he was relieved to learn that she was not with child in the end. He has settled a property and allowance on her, and Esmee has agreed to never return to London if Father does not turn her over for her crimes. In return, my father will handle all her medical needs in the future."

"That was kind of him," Edith said. "Does your father not wish to seek a divorce?"

He shook his head. "Sadly, or maybe thankfully, he has declared he does not intend to wed again."

"I think you gained your kind heart from him."

"A short month ago, I would have adamantly disagreed with you; however, upon recent introspection, I believe that to be true. I also believe I love you as deeply as he does Esmee."

"Which I can never think to be an objectionable trait." She risked a glance up at him. "Especially since that is what led you to me."

"To be candid, it was your undergarments that caught my eye long before I knew the beauty of your long, golden locks, amber eyes, and quick wit."

Edith swatted him with her free hand. "My lord!"

"But in all fairness, I have come to realize I love and adore you...almost as much as the sight of your knickers!" Triston's deep chuckle echoed through the room, drawing envious stares from lords and ladies alike.

"You are certainly lucky I love you in return...and can overlook your outrageous comments."

Ophelia and Luci motioned for them to follow as soon as they were almost upon them, before turning quickly and hurrying out onto the terrace.

Edith was helpless to do anything but trail the pair out the doors and into the refreshing night air. The moment she and Triston stepped over the threshold, Luci and Ophelia rounded on them.

"You will never guess who arrived only moments ago!" Ophelia nearly sang in delight.

"Who?" Edith inquired. She'd compiled the guest list and handwritten the invitations herself.

She made to look back into the ballroom to search the crowd for anyone who didn't belong.

"Do not look," Luci hissed. "He is coming this way, and he is certainly angry!"

"I can only imagine what trouble you ladies are embroiled in now." Triston scrutinized the woman. "However, this night belongs to Edith and me, and I will not have anything distracting me from her beauty and our future happiness."

With a grand flourish, he twirled Edith back toward the ballroom, his hand firmly at the small of her back, and guided her straight to the dance floor, giving her no opportunity to glance about to see who was headed for her friends on the terrace.

And it suited Edith marvelously as there was nothing she wanted more than to keep her attention on Triston.

Her friends could care for themselves for this one night.

"Triston," Edith sighed, relishing the warmth of his hold on her as they joined the other dancers' motion.

"Yes, my dearest ray of sunshine." He pulled her a few inches closer, and Edith allowed it. They were to be wed, after all, and who cared what gossip started now.

"Why do you call me that?" Edith bite her bottom lip when he smiled—that mischievous grin she'd come to adore.

"Do you remember the first time we met?"

"How could I forget, my lord? You saw my knickers before you knew my name." To Edith's great surprise her face did not flame with shame at the thought of her skirts tossed over her head due to her fall from the tree.

"Well, before I was afforded the handsome sight of your underpinnings, it was the reflection of the noonday sun off your golden hair that caught my notice."

"So, you are saying if I had my hood drawn, we might have never met?" she asked.

"My love." He shook his head as the final chord of music rang through the room. "Let us not ponder that possibility for then who would have been close to notice the disappearance of Lady Edith?"

"Perhaps there would have been no disappearance if…" Edith allowed her voice to trail off as Triston tucked her into his side once more and moved off the dance floor.

"Thankfully, there are only a few who know of your disappearance at all." He guided her toward a grouping of potted ferns, changing course when Lady Prudence and Lady Chastity came in to view. "My, my, Lady Edith, my dear sisters are determined to keep a close eye on you—however, I find myself in need of a kiss."

"Then you are lucky we did meet because I know the perfect place." Edith didn't hesitate before continuing through the potted ferns and along the wall, exiting out the servant's door that lead to the back staircase. "Come…"

AUTHOR'S NOTES

Thank you for reading *The Disappearance of Lady Edith
(The Undaunted Debutantes, Book One)*.

If you enjoyed *The Disappearance of Lady Edith*,
be sure to write a brief review at any retailer.

I'd love to hear from you!

You can contact me at:
Christina@christinamcknight.com

Or write me at:
P.O. Box 1017
Patterson, CA 95363

www.ChristinaMcKnight.com
Check out my website for giveaways, book reviews, and
information on my upcoming projects,
or connect with me through social media at:

Twitter: @CMcKnightWriter
Facebook: www.facebook.com/christinamcknightwriter
Goodreads: www.goodreads.com/ChristinaMcKnight

Sign up for my newsletter here:
http://eepurl.com/VP1rP

**For more information about The Undaunted
Debutantes, turn the page!**

THE UNDAUNTED DEBUTANTES

Three innocent debutantes must work to solve the mysterious death of their childhood friend. With undaunted determination they pledge to not only expose the man responsible for their friend's tragic death on her wedding night, but to also uncover other unscrupulous men of the *ton* who would jeopardize the future of other young women.

The Disappearance of Lady Edith
The Misfortune of Lady Lucianna
The Misadventures of Lady Ophelia

AVAILABLE IN PRINT AND E-BOOK

The Misfortune of Lady Lucianna
Book 2
Available June 13, 2017

Lady Lucianna Constantine, a quick-witted hellion, has no doubt who is responsible for the murder of her dear friend—and she will stop at nothing from exposing his transgressions, and those of every despicable man in London. Though her two dearest friends are unwilling to point a finger at the dastardly man, Lucianna has witnessed the cruelty of London's Beau Monde her entire life…starting with her own father. She is more than willing to singlehandedly take down every vile man that crosses her path. However, what happens when a most honorable man discovers Luci is the abhorrent woman who ruined both his life and stripped him of his rightful future?

The Misadventures of Lady Ophelia
Book 3
Available July 11, 2017

If only Lady Ophelia Fletcher—quiet, reserved, with her nose always stuck in a book—had witnessed the death of her friend that fateful night. Desperate to make amends for holding her tongue the night her dear friend was murdered, she now she writes a column, *Mayfair Confidential,* that she uses to expose men with unsavory pasts. But when a handsome stranger arrives to meet with her father, Ophelia can't help but do a little investigating for her own benefit. At last, she's stumbled upon an adventure of her own—but does she possess the skills necessary to solve the mystery without the assistance of her friends?

ABOUT THE AUTHOR

USA TODAY Bestselling Author Christina McKnight writes emotional and intricate Regency Romance with strong women and maverick heroes.

Her books combine romance and mystery, exploring themes of redemption and forgiveness. When she's not writing, Christina enjoys trying new coffeehouses, visiting wine bars, traveling the world, and watching television.

Email: Christina@ChristinaMcKnight.com
Follow her on Twitter: @CMcKnightWriter
Keep up to date on her releases:
www.christinamcknight.com
Like Christina's FB Author page:
ChristinaMcKnightWriter